CRESSIDA BLYTHEWOOD

The Duke's Secret

First edition

This book was professionally typeset on Reedsy.
Find out more at reedsy.com

Contents

1

A Vicious Lie

Callum

The heavy oak door of my study closed behind me, the sound a dull, final thud that sealed me in with the roaring in my own head. The silence of the room was absolute, a stark contrast to the tempest that had just been unleashed within me. I did not light a candle. I preferred the darkness. It was a more honest reflection of the state of my soul.

I walked to the decanter on the sideboard, my movements stiff, unnaturally precise. My hand was as steady as a rock as I poured a liberal measure of brandy into a heavy crystal tumbler. I was the Duke of Highmoor. My hands did not shake. My voice did not tremble. My face did not betray the fact that my entire world, a fragile, sunlit structure I had only just begun to believe in, had been razed to the ground in the space of a single, overheard conversation.

The fragments of her words echoed in my mind, sharp and lethal as broken glass. They played on a loop, a tormenting chorus of deceit.

"...You lied to me... You and my father... You told me I would never see... again..."

I had paused in the hallway, my hand raised to knock, intending to rescue her from her aunt's suffocating presence. I had stopped, arrested by the raw, ragged fury in her voice—a fury I had never heard from her before. And I had listened. An honorable man would have walked away. But I was no longer an honorable man. I was a husband, and I had heard my wife speaking of a profound, foundational lie.

"*...gone forever.*"

My mind, a cold, logical engine, seized on the phrases, trying to piece them into a coherent narrative. But my heart, that treacherous, newly awakened organ, was already bleeding. The specific pronoun she had used had been lost, swallowed by the thick wood of the door and her own emotional turmoil, but it did not matter. My own bitter history, a ghost I carried in my very bones, supplied the missing piece with a terrible, damning certainty.

Him. The "precious someone." The ghost from the chapel.

I tossed the brandy back in one raw, burning gulp, welcoming the fire that seared a path down my throat. It was a clean pain, a simple pain. It was nothing compared to the wound she had just inflicted. I had held her in my arms as she wept for him. I had offered her my patience, my understanding, my trust—a thing I had not given freely to any soul in five years. And it had all been based on a lie.

"*...you pushed me back into society... Did you plan this? Did you throw me in the Duke's path...?*"

The final, damning fragment clicked into place. My breath hitched. This was not just a story of a tragic lost love. This was a conspiracy. A cold, calculated game in which I was the grand prize, the unwitting pawn.

I stood by the window, the cool glass a useless balm against my heated forehead, and I began to assemble the pieces of the ugly, vicious truth. The truth they had hidden from me.

The "precious someone" she mourned was not dead. Her family had lied to her. They had told her he was gone forever, perhaps even that he had died, to force a severance, to push her towards a more advantageous match. Towards me. Her grief in the chapel was not for a memory, but for a living man she believed she could never have. Her sorrow at leaving Ravenswood was not for a place, but for a past she yearned for.

The memory of the chapel at Ravenswood returned to me then, sharp and sudden. I saw her standing in the candlelight, her face a mask of exquisite sorrow. I remembered her broken words—"*Someone very precious to me... and*

I... I lost..." At the time, moved by a foolish, burgeoning tenderness, I had assumed she meant he was dead. I had held her as she wept, offering her the comfort of a shared burden. What a blind fool I had been. I saw it now with a terrible clarity: it had been a performance, a masterpiece of manipulation. She had never said he was dead. She had said she *lost* him—a clever, deliberate choice of words to elicit my sympathy while hiding the damning truth. She had used her grief as a shield, weeping in my arms for a man who was very much alive, a man her family had simply taken from her.

And her retreat from me... Dear God. Her retreat after our night at the inn, after she had met my passion with a fire so real I had believed in it, believed in *us*... it was not fear. It was not regret. It was guilt.

The thought was a shard of ice in my gut, twisting with a jealousy so potent it was nauseating. She had lain in my arms, her body pliant and responsive, while her heart, her soul, belonged to another man. I had been a substitute. A necessary duty. A betrayal of a ghost.

The bitter taste of being made a fool of rose in my throat. It was a familiar taste, a poison I thought I had purged from my system years ago.

The pattern was the same. A beautiful woman with haunted eyes, a web of secrets, a core of deceit that revealed itself only after I had been foolish enough to trust. A cold, familiar dread, the ghost of a past I could never escape, coiled in my stomach. I saw Violetta's face then, as clearly as if she were standing in the room with me, her beautiful eyes full of lies, her lips curved in a smile that was a masterpiece of deception.

I remembered the night I had found the letters—not from a dead lover, but from a very living one. I remembered her cool, defiant denials, the beautiful lies that had dripped from her lips even as the proof was in my hand. I remembered the final, ugly truth: her tears, her hysterics, her tragic end, had all been a performance to cover her own profound, damning betrayal.

The memory was a physical agony, a phantom blade twisting in an old wound. I had been made a fool of once, in the most profound and humiliating way a man can be. I had sworn on Violetta's grave that it would never happen again. And yet, here I was. Another wife. Another secret lover. Another lie at the very heart of my marriage. The sheer, breathtaking cruelty of it, the

3

cosmic irony, threatened to shatter the last of my composure. It was as if fate itself had decided to punish me twice for the same sin of trust, sending me another beautiful, broken woman to complete the destruction the first had begun.

The fragile, tentative hope I had so foolishly allowed to take root in my heart was not just shattered; it was incinerated. The memory of the past weeks was now a source of deep, abiding shame. Her laughter by the pond, the gentle weight of her hand in mine, the soft, unguarded look on her face in the morning light at the inn—it had all been a performance. An exquisite, convincing, and utterly false performance. I had been weak. I had seen her sorrow and mistaken it for a vulnerability that mirrored my own. I had seen her strength and mistaken it for an honor I could rely upon. I had allowed her to breach my defenses, to make me feel tenderness, to make me feel hope.

I had been a fool.

I turned from the window and walked back to my desk, my movements once more calm and controlled. The storm of emotion had passed. In its place, the ice was returning, creeping back through my veins, thicker and colder than ever before, freezing the hollow space where my treacherous heart used to be. It was a familiar, painful comfort.

The war I thought I was fighting—against society, against my rivals, against the ghosts of my past—had been a child's game. The true war, the most dangerous war, had been brewing in silence, under my own roof, with the woman who bore my name.

My feelings for her, the warmth, the tenderness, the desperate, aching desire—they did not vanish. That was the true torture. They were still there, a painful, traitorous ache in my chest, now poisoned by suspicion and a profound sense of betrayal.

I sat down in the heavy leather chair, the cool material a familiar anchor in the wreckage of my emotions. The game had changed. The pieces on the board had been rearranged while I was staring foolishly at the sun.

I would not confront her. Not yet. To do so would be to show my hand, to reveal my weakness. I would not give her the satisfaction of knowing she had wounded me. No, I would play their game. I would be the perfect, attentive husband. I would watch her. I would listen.

I would uncover the truth of this lie. I would identify this secret man, this ghost who was not a ghost. And I would understand what game my wife and her manipulative aunt were truly playing.

I made a vow then, not in a moment of hot, angry passion, but in the cold, calculating silence of my study. I would unearth every last one of her secrets. I would protect my name, my honor, and the house of Redwyck from this conspiracy that had been woven around me.

I was no longer her potential confidant. I was no longer her protector.

I had become her silent, unknowing adversary. And I would not rest until I had won, no matter the cost to my own treacherous, broken heart.

2

Back to Square One

Marietta

I awoke the next morning to the familiar, cold emptiness of my own bed. The sun, a pale, watery thing, was already filtering through the tall windows of my bedchamber, but the warmth of it did not reach me. A profound chill had settled deep in my bones, a chill that had nothing to do with the morning air and everything to do with the man whose rooms were a hundred yards away, in the opposite wing of this cold, grand house.

The memory of the last two days was a chaotic, painful blur. My confrontation with my aunt, the shocking revelation of her calculated manipulations, had left me reeling. But it was the memory of Callum, of the desperate hope I had felt in his presence followed by the devastating weight of my own necessary deception, that truly haunted me.

His confession of care, the raw vulnerability in his eyes as he knelt before me, had been a glimpse of a future I had never dared to imagine. And I had met it with a kiss of farewell and a whispered excuse. I had pushed him away, not out of a lack of feeling, but because the weight of my secrets was a chasm I did not know how to bridge. I had chosen to protect my daughter, to protect his family's honor, by sacrificing the fragile, burgeoning hope for my own heart.

The choice had been necessary. The consequences, I was beginning to realize, were unbearable.

I had wept myself to sleep, my pillow damp with the silent, hopeless tears of a woman trapped in a labyrinth of her own making. And now, as I allowed Mrs. Finch to dress me in a gown of subdued grey silk, a color that perfectly matched the ashes of my hopes, a new, more immediate terror began to take root.

I had to face him.

I walked to the morning room with the slow, hesitant steps of a prisoner walking to her own execution. I did not know what I would find. Would he be angry? Would he press me for the truth I could not give him? Would he demand an explanation for the tears I had shed, for the sorrow I could not name?

The reality was so much worse than any of those possibilities.

He was already there, seated at the head of the table, a political dispatch held in one hand. He looked up as I entered, and the man I had knelt before yesterday, the man whose face had been a mask of raw, wounded vulnerability, was gone. Completely and utterly gone.

In his place was the Duke of Highmoor. The formidable, unreadable Duke of Ice. The wall was back, higher and thicker and colder than ever before. There was no flicker of warmth in his eyes, no trace of the man who had held me in the chapel, who had confessed that he cared for me. There was only a cool, impenetrable civility, a politeness so profound it was more cutting than any insult.

"Good morning, Duchess," he said, his voice a flat, formal monotone. He rose politely, a perfect gentleman, and remained standing until I had taken my seat at the far, distant end of the table. The gesture, which should have been one of respect, felt like a dismissal, a re-establishment of the vast, formal distance between us.

"Your Grace," I replied, my own voice a strained whisper. My heart, which had been a frantic, anxious thing, now settled into a cold, heavy stone in my chest.

He did not know of my conversation with my aunt; he couldn't possibly.

The true, complex source of my turmoil was a closed book to him. Therefore, his retreat, this sudden, brutal return to the coldness of our early days, could only be a reaction to one thing: my rejection of him. He had laid his heart at my feet, and I had turned away. This was his response. A quiet, punishing, and absolute withdrawal born of wounded pride.

The silence that fell was not the charged, curious silence of the past few weeks. It was the dead, empty silence of a tomb. We ate, two strangers separated by an expanse of polished mahogany, attended by silent footmen who seemed acutely, painfully aware that the fragile truce between their master and mistress had been shattered.

Surely, I thought, this could not stand. His pride was wounded, yes, but the connection we had forged, the tenderness I had seen in his eyes, could not have been an illusion. Perhaps if I reached out, if I made the first move to bridge this new, icy gap, I could coax the man from the chapel back out from behind the Duke's formidable armor. I searched for something to say, anything to break the unbearable tension, to test the thickness of this new wall between us.

"The storm seems to have passed," I murmured, my gaze on the window, where the weak sun was attempting to break through the clouds. It was a foolish, desperate echo of the conversation that had begun our brief, beautiful journey into intimacy at the inn.

"Indeed," he replied, not looking up from his dispatch.

The single word, so clipped and final, was a door slamming shut in my face. Still, I refused to be so easily deterred. I tried again, choosing a topic I knew was a source of warmth for him, a shared and happy memory.

"I received a letter from your aunt this morning," I said, my voice a little brighter, a little more determined. "She writes that she is well, and sends her love. She told me about Isabelle and says that the child had a new pony."

At the mention of Isabelle, he froze for a fraction of a second. The hand holding the dispatch went utterly still. A look of such cold, profound displeasure passed over his features that it stole the very air from my lungs. It was gone as quickly as it came, replaced by that same mask of icy indifference, but I had seen it.

"That is good of her," he said, his voice flat and devoid of all interest. He pointedly turned the page of his dispatch, the crisp rustle of the paper a sound of absolute, final dismissal.

I failed. Miserably. The rejection was so complete, so utterly devastating, it left no room for another attempt. This was not just wounded pride. This was something deeper, colder, and more absolute. He had not just closed the door on any personal communication; he had locked it, bolted it, and thrown away the key.

I am once again the Duchess, a political necessity, and nothing more. The realization was a quiet, devastating agony.

I spent the rest of the meal staring at my plate, the food tasteless in my mouth, the weight of my failure a physical presence in the room. The dream of Ravenswood, the warmth of the inn, the hope that had been born in the chapel—it had all been a fleeting, beautiful illusion. This, this cold and silent distance, was my reality.

The silence after breakfast was a tomb. I rose from my chair, my own meal barely touched, and he did not even lift his eyes from his dispatch. There was no polite nod, no formal acknowledgment of my departure. I was simply dismissed, an empty chair at the far end of his table. I walked from the room, the sound of my own footsteps echoing in the vast, empty hall, feeling the weight of his indifference like a physical cloak on my shoulders.

The hours of the day stretched before me, a barren and desolate landscape. I retreated to my sitting room, a space that was supposed to be my sanctuary, but it felt like just another corner of my gilded cage. I picked up my embroidery, the needle feeling clumsy and foreign in my fingers, and set a few crooked stitches before letting it fall back into my lap. The silence of the house was absolute, broken only by the mournful ticking of the grandfather clock in the hall, each tick a slow, measured beat counting out the seconds of my lonely sentence.

Later, I stood by the window, watching a fine mist of rain bead on the glass, blurring the manicured gardens into a watercolor of grey and green. I saw him cross the lawn towards the stables, his long, powerful strides eating up the ground. He looked every inch the Duke, a man of purpose and authority, a master of his world. A world in which I was a stranger, a ghost at the window, watching a life I was not a part of.

The agony of it was a constant, low-grade fever. My mind would betray me, replaying the memory of our night at the inn, of his laughter on the journey from Ravenswood, of his hand holding mine. Had I imagined it all? Had that brief, beautiful warmth been nothing more than a fleeting mirage in the desert of our arrangement?

Dinner was a fresh torment, a formal and exquisitely cruel performance of our separation. I would sit at my end of the long, gleaming table, he at his, the vast expanse of polished mahogany between us a physical representation of the chasm that had opened in our lives. A dozen candles would burn in the silver candelabra, their light glinting off the crystal and porcelain, illuminating a feast I could not eat.

He would not speak. He would eat with a mechanical, detached precision, his gaze fixed on his plate or on a political dispatch propped against the wine decanter. The footmen would move between us, their faces impassive masks, their silence a testament to the cold, dead atmosphere in the room. They served the soup, the fish, the roasted pheasant, their movements a silent, well-rehearsed ballet of ducal duty. And I would sit there, a silent, perfectly dressed doll, the food tasteless in my mouth, the wine like ash on my tongue.

After the final course, he would rise, offer a curt, almost imperceptible bow in my direction, and retreat to his study without a word. The heavy oak door would close behind him, a sound of absolute, damning finality. He was gone, locked away in his world of politics and power, and I was left alone in the vast, echoing dining room, a queen in an empty kingdom.

The nights were the worst. There was no question of marital duty; the very idea was a bitter, mocking joke. Our wings of the house were separate countries with closed borders. My maid would help me prepare for bed, the ritual of unlacing my gown and brushing out my hair a silent, impersonal affair. She would leave, and I would be left alone in the vast, cold emptiness of my bedchamber. The bed, large enough for a king and his court, felt like a desolate, lonely island. I would lie awake for hours, staring into the darkness, listening. Listening for a footstep in the hall, for the turn of a doorknob, for any sign that the man I had married, the man I had given my body to, might seek me out. But the only sound was the beating of my own, lonely heart.

It was on one such evening, about a week after our return, that the silence became unbearable. He had retreated to his study immediately after dinner, as was his new custom. I could not face the cold solitude of my chambers. I found myself drawn, as if by an invisible thread, to the library, the scene of our first, accidental embrace, the memory of it a fresh, sharp pain.

I was standing by the shelves, a book of poetry held unread in my hand, when he entered. He had come for a folio, and he clearly had not expected to find me there. He stopped in the doorway, and for a moment, the carefully constructed masks we both wore seemed to slip. I saw a flicker of something in his eyes—a raw, unguarded look of longing and of pain—and I knew, with a sudden, heartbreaking certainty, that he was just as miserable in this cold war as I was. But the moment passed as quickly as it came. He gave me a curt, formal nod, retrieved the folio he had come for, and turned to leave without a word.

He was halfway to the door when I spoke his name.

"Callum."

The sound of it, a soft, desperate whisper in the quiet, cavernous room, seemed to hang in the air between us.

He stopped, his back to me. He did not turn.

"Is something amiss, Your Grace?" I asked, my voice trembling slightly. "You have seemed... distant since our return."

"I am merely occupied with matters of business," he replied, his voice a flat, cold thing that offered no room for further inquiry. It was a clear, polite dismissal. The finality in his tone, the wall he had so deliberately placed between us, was almost too much to bear.

"Have I... have I done something to displease you?" I pressed, my voice smaller now, full of a confusion I could no longer hide.

He was silent for a moment before answering, his back still to me. "No."

The single, clipped word was more painful than any tirade. My composure shattered.

"Please," I whispered, my voice breaking. "Do not let it be like this. If there

11

is some trouble between us, some offense I have given without knowing, I beg you, tell me what it is."

He turned then, slowly, and the look on his face was not of anger, but of a profound and weary sadness that was somehow more terrifying. "You wish for honesty, Marietta?" he asked, his voice dangerously quiet. "Then answer me this. Have you been entirely honest with me?"

The question was a trap, and I had walked right into it. I thought of Isabelle. I thought of the child growing within me. My throat closed, and I could not speak. I could only stare at him, my silence a damning confession to a crime he did not even understand.

A humorless, heartbreaking sigh escaped his lips. He looked at me, his eyes full of a weary resignation, and gave a single, almost imperceptible nod, as if accepting a verdict he had long dreaded.

"So be it," he said softly, the words a quiet surrender. "Keep your secrets, Duchess. But know this..."

He held my gaze, and the last of the warmth I had seen at Ravenswood was extinguished, leaving only a cold, bleak emptiness. "I cannot live on the scraps of a heart that belongs to another."

He turned then, his intention to leave absolute. The finality of his words, the sheer, baffling injustice of them, struck me into a state of stunned disbelief. *Another?* What other? My heart, a foolish and frozen thing for so long, had only just begun to thaw for *him.*

"What do you mean?" I asked, the words a choked, desperate plea to his retreating back. "Callum, what other are you speaking of?"

He stopped again, just at the threshold, but he did not turn. I could see the rigid, unyielding line of his shoulders, the way his hands were clenched into fists at his sides. The silence stretched between us, thick and heavy with his unspoken, damning judgment. He would not give me the dignity of an explanation. He had pronounced his sentence and was now walking away from the execution.

Without another word, he was gone, the heavy oak door closing with a soft, final click behind him.

I was left alone in the silent, shadowed library, his words a baffling and painful riddle. What did he mean, a heart belonging to another?

My mind raced, grasping for an explanation, but every path led back to the same desolate place: my own past. Had he heard some fresh, vicious piece of gossip? Had the full, sordid reality of my ruin finally become too much for his pride to bear?

Perhaps that was what he meant—that my heart, in his eyes, would always belong to my own shame. He was not just rejecting me; he was rejecting the scandal I embodied.

I was left with the chilling certainty that the ghost he could not live with was not another man, but the woman I used to be, and the full, crushing weight of a truth I could never tell.

3

The Price of Silence

Marietta

The silence in the dining room was a weapon. For the past week, it had been my husband's chosen instrument of torture, a cold, sharp blade he wielded with devastating precision. We sat at opposite ends of the vast, gleaming table, two solitary figures in a sea of polished mahogany and flickering candlelight. The footmen moved around us like ghosts, their soft footsteps the only sound to break the profound, suffocating quiet that had become my new reality.

Every night was the same. He would be impeccably polite, his voice a cool, formal monotone as he requested the salt or commented on the wine. His eyes, those pale grey shards of ice, would look at me but not see me. He saw only a stranger, a ghost of the woman he had held in his arms, and the distance in his gaze was a constant, painful rejection.

I could not bear it. The memory of our night at the inn, of the warmth of his body and the shocking, beautiful intimacy we had shared, was a constant, tormenting counterpoint to this new, brutal reality. I had replayed his words from the library a thousand times in the lonely darkness of my room. *A heart that belongs to another.* The accusation made no sense, yet it was the rock upon which our fragile truce had shattered. I could only conclude that he had decided the scandal of my past was a ghost too powerful to live with; that he regretted our marriage and was now retreating behind the impenetrable walls of his ducal title.

Tonight, the tension was different. It was not a cold, dead thing; it was a live wire, humming in the space between us. I could feel his gaze on me, even when my own eyes were fixed on my plate. It was a sharp, analytical scrutiny, the look of a man trying to solve a puzzle that infuriated him. The air crackled with his unspoken frustration, and with every passing, silent minute, I felt my own composure begin to fray.

As the footmen cleared the final course and retreated, a sense of finality settled over the room. Callum placed his napkin beside his plate. He pushed his chair back, the sound a harsh scrape against the marble floor, and rose, preparing to make his customary escape to the solitude of his study.

The finality of the gesture, the promise of another long, silent, lonely night stretching before me, was too much to bear. A desperate courage, born of heartbreak and a sliver of lingering hope, rose in me.

"Callum," I said, my voice quiet but clear, stopping him in his tracks.

He froze, his back to me, a formidable, unmoving silhouette.

"Please," I whispered, my voice breaking. "Do not leave. Not like this. Can we not... speak?"

For a long, agonizing moment, he did not move. Then, slowly, he turned. The polite mask was gone. His face was a mask of cold, controlled fury, and his eyes were blazing.

"Speak?" he repeated, the word a low, dangerous thing. "You wish for us to speak?" He took a step away from the door, back towards the table. "Then tell me, Marietta, was it all a performance? The inn? The afternoon in the park? Are you so skilled in the art of deception that you can offer your body while your heart remains locked away with a ghost?"

The accusation, so brutal and so specific, referencing the intimacy I had cherished, stole the air from my lungs. "A ghost?" I whispered, shaking my head. "The past is the past, Callum. Why must you insist on giving it life?"

"Do not play the innocent with me!" he snapped, his voice a low, vicious growl. He started walking towards me then, down the long, intimidating length of the table. "His name is still on every tongue in this city. *Thorne.* They speak of him as if he were still here. Is he? Is that the truth you are hiding? That you are married to me in name, but shackled to him in spirit?"

His words struck me with the force of a physical blow. I was genuinely baffled, my mind reeling to comprehend the direction of his fury. Thorne? A ghost from a lifetime ago. How could he possibly believe...

"What do you mean?" I whispered, the question a breath of pure, unadulterated confusion. "Shackled to him? He is nothing to me."

My denial, which was the absolute truth, only seemed to enrage him further. He saw it as a lie, an insult to his intelligence. "Do not," he hissed, his voice dropping to a dangerous whisper as he drew closer, "play me for a fool. I see the way you look when you believe no one is watching. Every sad look, every secret tear—it is for him. Your heart is not a mystery to me, Marietta."

He had reached my chair. He stood over me, his presence a dark, overwhelming shadow. He leaned down, placing his hands on the arms of my chair, trapping me. I could feel the heat of his anger, see the frantic, wounded pulse beating in his throat.

"You are twisting everything," I said, my voice trembling, but I forced it to be firm. "This has nothing to do with a memory. The truth... the truth is a burden I carry for the sake of others. For the sake of peace. Please, I beg you, do not force this. You will unleash a sorrow that will destroy us all."

Words had failed us. His fury, born of a lie he believed, and my terror, born of a truth I could not tell, met in the space between us, leaving no room for reason. There was only one way to silence the storm.

"Then we don't need to talk," he growled, but instead of pulling me to him, he turned as if to leave, a gesture of absolute, final dismissal.

The thought of him walking away, leaving us in this state of cold, angry ruin, was more than I could bear. "No, Callum, please," I pleaded, taking a step after him. "Let us speak of this. Truly speak. There is a misunderstanding."

He stopped and turned back slowly, his eyes blazing with a cold, wounded fire. "A misunderstanding?" he repeated, his voice dangerously quiet. "Then clarify it for me. Tell me the secret you have been hiding. The name of the man whose memory you so clearly cherish. Tell me everything, Marietta.

Now."

His demand was an impossible ultimatum. I could not tell him the truth—not the real truth of Isabelle, not the truth of the new life I carried. I could only deflect, a desperate attempt to protect them both. "My sorrows are my own," I whispered, my voice trembling. "They have nothing to do with you, or with us."

The finality of my refusal, my inability to give him the answer he demanded, seemed to shatter the last of his control. A chilling smile, devoid of all humor, touched his lips. "So, the Duchess refuses to speak to her husband," he murmured, his voice a low, mocking caress as he closed the distance between us. He leaned closer, his lips brushing my ear as he whispered the final, devastating question. "Does she also refuse to lie with him?"

The crude, possessive question shattered the last of my resistance. I knew then that arguing was pointless. He was not a man to be reasoned with. He was a proud, wounded Duke, consumed by a jealous rage I could not comprehend and could not fight with words. To continue to refuse him would only lead to a different, colder kind of cruelty. And in the deepest, most secret corner of my heart, a part of me that had been starved for his touch ached to surrender.

A single tear I could no longer hold back escaped, tracing a hot path down my cheek. I stopped struggling, my body going still in his grasp. I lifted my gaze to meet his, my own eyes a turbulent storm of heartbreak and a desperate, dawning surrender.

"No," I whispered, my voice breaking on the single word. "She does not refuse."

My whispered consent, a confession of both defeat and desire, was the only answer he needed. The fire in his eyes changed, the sharp edges of anger consumed by a raw, overwhelming hunger. The storm of our argument had finally, irrevocably, broken.

He did not give me a moment to reconsider. His mouth claimed mine, not with the bruising assault I had feared, but with a desperate intensity that was all-consuming. It was a kiss that sealed my surrender. And with a low, wounded sound, a sob that he swallowed with his own lips, I melted against him. I responded with a fervor that matched his own, a wild, desperate hunger that stole the air from my lungs. All my sorrow, all my loneliness, all my frustrated longing poured into that kiss. My hands, which had been pushing him away, slid up his chest to tangle in his hair, pulling his head down, deepening the kiss until it was a raw, open-mouthed battle of tongues and teeth and breath.

The fire of our argument transformed into a different kind of inferno. The anger burned away, leaving only a raw, desperate desire. We were just two lonely, wounded souls, clinging to each other in the dark as if seeking a solace we could not find in words.

He broke the kiss only to groan my name against my lips. "Marietta," he breathed, and then his mouth was on my throat, my collarbone, the sensitive skin of my neck. I cried out, my head falling back, a willing sacrifice to his sudden, all-consuming hunger. This was not the gentle man from the library, nor the cold Duke. This was a man of fire and impulse, and I, who had lived in a world of ice for so long, welcomed the burn.

His hands were frantic, tearing at the laces of my evening gown. I was just as desperate, my trembling fingers fumbling with the buttons of his waistcoat, needing to feel the warmth of his skin against mine. Clothes were a prison, and we were staging a violent, passionate escape.

He shrugged out of his coat and waistcoat. I worked at the buttons of his shirt, my knuckles brushing against the hard wall of his chest. The moment my palms finally met his bare skin, a collective shudder ran through us both. He was hot to the touch, his muscles hard and corded.

He lifted his head, his eyes blazing with a dark, possessive fire. In his gaze, I saw not anger, not frustration, but a raw, undisguised wanting that stole the very breath from my lungs. With a low groan, he lifted me as if I weighed nothing. My body, acting on instinct, wrapped my legs around his waist. He carried me from the dining room, his mouth never leaving mine, kicking open doors as we went.

He did not take me to my chamber. He took me to his. He laid me down on the vast, dark expanse of his bed, the fine linen cool against my heated skin. He followed me down, his weight a welcome, possessive pressure. He pushed the thin fabric of my chemise aside, the cool night air on my bared skin a shock, quickly replaced by the heat of his gaze. He looked at my breasts as if he were a starving man and they were a feast.

"Beautiful," he rasped, and then he lowered his head.

The moment his mouth closed over my nipple, my entire world shattered into a million points of pure, white-hot pleasure. I cried out, my back arching off the bed, my fingers digging into his broad shoulders. He suckled, his tongue laving the sensitive peak, sending bolts of lightning straight to the core of me, to the empty, aching place between my legs. He was merciless, worshiping one breast and then the other, until I was a writhing, whimpering creature beneath him.

He moved lower, his mouth and hands trailing a path of fire over my ribs, my waist. His hand slid down, over my belly. His fingers tangled in the dark curls there, and then he found me. His thumb brushed over the small, hidden nub of my sex, and a scream of pure, unadulterated shock and pleasure tore from my throat. He explored me with a slow, devastating confidence, his fingers stroking, circling, learning the slick, wet heat of my desire. I was panting, sobbing, my hips arching off the bed to meet his touch.

He shifted, positioning himself between my legs, the hard, thick length of him pressing against my wet heat. "Marietta," he whispered, his voice a raw, broken thing. "Look at me."

I forced my heavy eyelids open. He was watching me, his face a mask of intense, almost painful concentration, his grey eyes dark with a passion so profound it was humbling.

"I have never," he said, his voice a low, rough rasp, "needed anyone as I need you. Now."

He entered me then, not with a rush, but with a slow, deliberate pressure, stretching me, filling me, until he was seated deep inside me. I gasped, my body accepting him, the feeling of him inside me a dizzying, overwhelming sensation of completeness. For the first time in my life, I felt not empty, but full.

He began to move, a slow, deep rhythm that was both a claiming and a worship. Every thrust was a question, and my arching hips were the answer. The pleasure built, a relentless, rising tide, until I was clinging to him, my

19

nails scoring his back, my world narrowing to the feel of his body inside mine.

"Callum," I cried out, and at the sound of his name on my lips, he shuddered, his own control breaking. His thrusts became deeper, faster, harder, driving us both towards the precipice. I fell first, my body convulsing around him in a wave of pure, shattering ecstasy. I heard my own voice cry out his name again, a sound of pure release. He followed a moment later, his body going rigid, a low, guttural groan tearing from his throat as he emptied himself deep inside me.

In the aftermath, we lay tangled together, our bodies slick with sweat, our breathing harsh in the quiet room. He collapsed beside me but did not withdraw. He simply held me, his heart hammering against my ear.

The fire of our anger and passion had been spent, leaving behind only the cold ashes of our unresolved conflict. There was no tenderness in his touch now, no gentle stroking of my hair. He lay beside me, a rigid, silent stranger once more, his arm a heavy, possessive weight, but not a comforting one. The storm had passed through us, a violent, beautiful, and ultimately meaningless cataclysm. It had not cleared the air. It had only left devastation in its wake, and the silence that descended was deeper, more profound, and more hopeless than any that had come before.

4

A Fragile Façade

Marietta

I learned that there are many kinds of silence. There is the hostile, empty silence of a new and unwanted arrangement. There is the charged, electric silence that precedes a storm. And then there is this, the worst of them all: the dead, hollow silence of the morning after.

The night of our argument did not clear the air. It had been a wildfire, a conflagration that burned away the last of our fragile pretenses and left only scorched, barren earth behind. We had bared our bodies, but our souls remained locked away, more fiercely guarded than ever. He had taken me to his bed, an act of possession and desperation, but he had not invited me into his life. The moment the act was over, the wall of ice had returned, thicker and more impenetrable than before, fortified now by the memory of a passion that had solved nothing. I had woken alone in his vast, cold bed, the space beside me already empty, the only evidence of his presence the faint, masculine scent on the pillows and the deeper, more profound ache in my own heart.

We settled into a new, cold routine, a fragile façade of a marriage that was, I believe, the most convincing performance of my life. To the outside world, to the watchful, ever-judging eyes of the *ton*, we were the perfect Duke and Duchess. We were a success. The initial scandal of our hasty union had been smoothed over, replaced by a grudging, wary respect. We were a power couple, a united front, his formidable presence complemented by my serene, quiet grace.

The performance was flawless because we were both exquisitely motivated. He, to protect the honor of his name; I, to protect myself from the unbearable reality of my own choices. It was a role we played not just for the watchful eyes of the *ton*, but for our own staff, a silent, daily charade that began long before we ever left the house. The stage was set every afternoon at four o'clock, when the ducal carriage was brought around for the obligatory drive.

"His Grace is waiting in the hall, Your Grace," my maid would inform me, and I would take one last, steadying breath before the mirror, composing my features into a mask of serene contentment.

I would descend the grand staircase to find him there, always impeccably dressed, his expression one of cool neutrality. He would offer me his arm for the short walk to the front doors, the gesture a perfect pantomime of husbandly attentiveness. I would place my hand on his sleeve, feeling the hard, unyielding muscle beneath the fine wool, and we would proceed through the hall, two elegant strangers performing for an audience of silent, liveried footmen.

He would offer me his hand to help me into the carriage, his touch firm and correct, his fingers brushing mine for a fraction of a second before retreating. The brief contact was a torment, a phantom limb of the intimacy we had shared and then annihilated.

The short journey to the park was conducted in our now-customary silence. Only when our carriage joined the slow, fashionable procession at Hyde Park did the next act of the performance truly begin. I would take my seat opposite him, the space between us a yawning chasm of unspoken words, and we would turn our faces to the world.

Outside, the park was a swirl of color and life. Fashionable ladies preened in their open landaus, gentlemen trotted by on gleaming thoroughbreds, and the air was filled with the bright, brittle sound of society's laughter. Inside our carriage, the silence was a tangible thing, broken only by the necessities of our public role.

"Lady Danbury appears to have acquired a new set of matched greys," he might observe, his gaze fixed on a carriage passing ours, his voice pitched just loud enough for any nearby driver to hear.

"They are very fine," I would reply, my voice a soft, steady thing that cost me a great deal of effort, my own smile directed at the world outside my window.

And that would be the extent of it. He would look out his window, and I would look out mine. But I was not seeing the parade of fashion. I was seeing the ghost of our journey from Ravenswood, the memory of his easy laughter, of his hand holding mine. I remembered the stories he had told, the glimpses of the boy he had been. Where was that man now? Had I imagined him? Had I killed him with my own secrets and sorrows?

It was on one of these drives, while smiling serenely at a passing acquaintance, that the fatigue first washed over me. It was a weariness so bone-deep, so profound, that the simple act of maintaining my posture felt like a Herculean effort. My smile felt heavy on my face, the pearl necklace at my throat a leaden weight. I wanted nothing more than to close my eyes, to lean my head back against the velvet squabs and surrender to the encroaching grey fog. I blamed the late nights, the sleepless hours spent staring into the darkness, my mind a relentless whirlwind of what-ifs and regrets. The strain of the performance was simply taking its toll.

The evenings were a different kind of performance, a more intimate and thus more agonizing one. In private, the pretense of conversation ceased entirely. We would sit at opposite ends of that vast, gleaming dining table, the distance between us a physical manifestation of our emotional chasm. The footmen moved around us like ghosts, their soft footsteps the only sound to break the profound, suffocating quiet. He would read his political dispatches between courses, his attention absolute, effectively erasing my presence from the room.

I watched him one night over the rim of my wine glass. The candlelight caught the sharp, elegant lines of his face, making him look like a formidable Roman statue, all cool marble and unyielding strength. There was no trace of the passionate, desperate man who had torn at my clothes, whose mouth had worshiped my body. There was no trace of the vulnerable man who had knelt at my feet and confessed that he cared. There was only the Duke. Cold. Controlled. Distant.

It was on that night that the nausea first stirred. The rich scent of the roasted duck, which normally would have been appealing, was suddenly overwhelming, cloying. A wave of queasiness rose in my throat, and I hastily placed my wine glass down, my hand trembling slightly. I took a small, discreet sip of water, focusing on the intricate pattern of the damask tablecloth, breathing slowly until the feeling subsided. I pushed the food around on my plate for the rest of the meal, my appetite gone.

Across the table, Callum looked up from his papers, his grey eyes narrowing for a fraction of a second as he took in my untouched plate. He placed his dispatch down on the table with a quiet, deliberate finality.

"Is the food not to your liking, Duchess?" he asked.

His voice was a flat, cool instrument, utterly devoid of warmth. It was not the question of a concerned husband, but of a master of a house noting a potential complaint. The query was not about my well-being, but about the quality of his cook's offerings.

"Forgive me, Your Grace," I murmured, not meeting his gaze. "The cook has outdone himself, as always. I find I am simply without an appetite this evening."

He gave a single, sharp nod of acknowledgement, a gesture that was both an acceptance and a dismissal. He immediately picked his papers back up, his attention already returned to a report on trade tariffs, leaving me in a silence that was now thick with my own humiliation. His duty was done; he had inquired. He had no interest in the cause. It was a cool, analytical assessment, the look of a man noting a flaw in a piece of machinery, and I felt my heart settle into a cold, heavy stone in my chest.

My days were a performance. And the nights... the nights were a torment of a different, more intimate kind. The ducal line required an heir, and my husband was a man who did not shirk his responsibilities. He would come to my chambers some nights, a silent, formidable shadow in the candlelight. There were no tender words, no lingering kisses that spoke of the man I had known at the inn. Our encounters were silent, efficient acts of necessity, a duty performed in the vast, lonely darkness of my bed.

I would lie there, my body a willing traitor that responded to his touch, while my heart screamed in the silence. I understood his coldness now, the source of the suspicion that had returned with such force after the Ashworths' supper. It was Julian Thorne. He believed my heart was still entangled with the ghost of a poet, that my secret grief was for a living rival. A part of me, a small, desperate voice, screamed that I should tell him the truth—at least that part of it. It would be so easy to say, *"He is nothing to me, Callum. A foolish girl's mistake from a lifetime ago."* It would be so easy to clear away that one, simple misunderstanding.

But I knew, with a certainty that chilled me to the bone, that those words would only be the first step on a path to ruin. His next question would be inevitable: *"Then what is the secret, Marietta? What is the source of your sorrow?"*

And to answer that would be to speak of a secret birth, of a child given away, of a daughter now living under his own family's protection. To tell the truth about Julian would be to light a fuse that led directly to Isabelle. I knew my silence was poisoning the fragile trust between us, that it was cementing his belief in my deception. But to speak, to risk even the slightest chance of a scandal that could destroy Isabelle's future... that was a price I was not willing to pay. My daughter's safety was paramount. My own chance at happiness, and my husband's peace of mind, had to come second. The choice was a silent, daily agony.

Having made my lonely, heartbreaking decision to remain silent, a fresh wave of sorrow washed over me for the man I was forced to deceive. And so, with the weight of my lie heavy on my soul, I would search his face in the dim light for a flicker of the man from our stolen afternoon, the man who had looked at me with such raw, desperate need. I was looking for a sign that the kind, passionate man I had glimpsed still existed beneath the cold armor, even as I knew my own secrecy was helping to keep him locked away. But there was only the cool, impersonal focus of the Duke, ensuring the continuation of his lineage.

And afterward, he would withdraw, both physically and emotionally, with a quiet finality that was more cutting than any cruel word. He would dress in the shadows and be gone without looking back, leaving me alone in the tangled sheets, the scent of him a cruel reminder of the chasm that lay between us. It was in those moments, in the cold, empty space he left behind, that the longing was the worst. A longing for a daughter I could not claim and a husband I could not truly reach.

It was no wonder my constitution was beginning to suffer. The body, after all, could only endure what the heart could bear, and my heart was breaking.

The library, once my sanctuary, became another stage for my secret turmoil. I retreated there one afternoon, desperate for a moment of quiet, for the comforting scent of old leather and beeswax. I was attempting to reply to a stack of invitations that had accumulated on my secretary, but the elegant script blurred before my eyes. The room, which I had once found so peaceful, now felt claustrophobic, the towering shelves of books like silent, judging witnesses to my unhappiness.

A wave of dizziness, swift and sudden, washed over me. The world tilted, the edges of the room softening into a hazy, indistinct watercolor. A high, ringing sound filled my ears, and I gripped the edge of the heavy mahogany desk, my knuckles turning white, my breath catching in a panicked gasp. I was falling. I closed my eyes, praying I would not faint, not here, not alone where I might not be found for hours.

The moment passed as quickly as it came, leaving me trembling and slick with a cold sweat. I pressed the back of my hand to my forehead. It was clammy. I was simply exhausted. I was not sleeping well. I was not eating properly. My life was a lie, and the strain of it was manifesting in these small, physical rebellions.

A cold, familiar dread coiled in the pit of my stomach. This weariness, this sudden aversion to scents, the faint but persistent nausea in the mornings—I knew these feelings. I had known them intimately in another lifetime, in a lonely summer manor in Northumberland. My body was sending me signals I recognized, ghosts of a past I had tried so desperately to bury.

But I refused. I would not acknowledge it. It was nothing more than a cruel trick of memory, my own grief twisting my body into a phantom echo of what had come before. It could not be anything more.

I refused to entertain the other possibility, the one that flickered at the very back of my mind, a tiny, terrifying spark of hope and of dread. The night in his bed, the fierce, desperate, and ultimately fruitless passion we had shared—it had been a singular event, a storm that had passed, leaving no trace behind. It could not have... taken root. Not now. Not in the midst of this desolate, emotional wasteland. To be with child, to be carrying my husband's heir in a marriage that was a barren, loveless sham, would be an irony so cruel, so profound, I did not think my heart could bear it.

The thought of bringing another child into this web of secrets was horrifying. How could I welcome a new life when my firstborn was a ghost I could only visit in my dreams? How could I offer a child a home that was not a home, but a battleground of silent, wounded pride?

And so I dismissed it. I pushed the thought away with a fierce, desperate denial. It was stress. It was exhaustion. It was grief. It was anything and everything but the one, impossible, world-altering truth that I was too afraid to even whisper in the silent, lonely darkness of my own heart. I was the Duchess of Highmoor, and my only duty was to maintain the façade, no matter how fragile it had become.

5

Whispers of the Past

Callum

Duty, in our world, was a relentless creditor. It cared nothing for the silent wars waged in the private chambers of a man's home. It demanded its due. And so, a fortnight after our return to the city, duty demanded our presence at a political supper hosted by Lord and Lady Fitzgibbon. Fitzgibbon was a key ally, his support in the upcoming parliamentary session crucial, and my absence would have been noted, dissected, and used as a weapon by my enemies.

I stood before the pier glass in my dressing room, my valet making the final, precise adjustments to my cravat. I saw not my own reflection, but the hollow-eyed stranger I had become in the past weeks. The fragile hope that had taken root at Ravenswood had been systematically starved, leaving behind the familiar, bitter taste of disappointment. I had retreated behind my wall of ice, and she behind hers. Our home was a fortress of two opposing, silent armies, and the only ground we shared was the public stage.

Tonight was another such stage.

When I met her at the top of the grand staircase, she was a vision in a gown of deep midnight blue that made her skin look like alabaster and her eyes like shadowed emeralds. The Redwyck diamonds glittered at her throat, a cold, beautiful fire. She was the perfect Duchess, a creature of serene, untouchable grace. There was no trace of the laughing woman who had held my hand in the carriage, no sign of the passionate, desperate creature who had met my anger with a fire of her own. She was a stranger, and she was my wife.

"You look magnificent, Duchess," I said, my voice the cool, formal instrument I now used with her.

"Thank you, Your Grace," she replied, her own voice a soft, distant melody. She placed her gloved hand on my offered arm, her touch as light and as fleeting as a whisper.

Fitzgibbon's London house was ablaze with light, the air thick with the scent of melted wax, expensive perfume, and political ambition. We moved through the crowded rooms, a seamless unit, the Duke and Duchess of Highmoor, a portrait of unified power. I guided her through the throng, my hand a correct, formal presence at the small of her back. I engaged in conversation with ministers and their wives, my mind sharp, my observations incisive. And all the while, a part of my attention was fixed on her.

She was playing her part to perfection. She smiled, she murmured polite responses, she was the very picture of ducal serenity. But I, who had become an unwilling scholar of her moods, could see the strain beneath the surface. I saw the faint, bruised shadows under her eyes that no amount of powder could completely conceal, the slight, almost imperceptible tremor in her hand as she lifted a champagne flute to her lips. The woman was suffering, and the sight of it was a constant, low-grade torment, a reminder of the chasm of secrets that lay between us.

It was after supper, while the ladies were gathered in one knot and the men in another, that the past chose to resurrect itself. I was engaged in a tedious but necessary conversation with a trio of backbenchers about trade tariffs when I saw Lady Pembroke descend upon my wife. Pembroke was a woman whose wit was surpassed only by her malice, a creature who delighted in the discomfort of others. I watched her, a prickle of unease tightening the muscles in my neck.

Marietta was seated on a small settee, and Lady Pembroke sat beside her, her head bent in a gesture of false, conspiratorial intimacy. I was too far away to hear their words, but I saw the exchange. I saw Lady Pembroke's sly, knowing smile, and I saw the subtle, almost imperceptible stiffening of my wife's spine. I saw the polite, meaningless smile on Marietta's face become a little more brittle, her hands clenching in her lap.

My conversation with the backbenchers faded to a dull drone. My focus narrowed. At that moment, two older gentlemen passed behind me, their voices a low, rumbling murmur.

"...Thorne, I believe the name was," the first one said, his tone laced with the smug satisfaction of a man sharing a juicy piece of gossip. "A poet of some minor repute, though more for his debts than his couplets."

The name struck me like a physical blow. *Julian Thorne.* The poet. The man who had caused my wife's ruin. The ghost I had accused her of loving.

"A complete scoundrel," the second man agreed with a chuckle. "Ran off to the continent with a mountain of debt and a sullied reputation. Chased half the married women in London. They say he was utterly shameless. Ruined that young Greystone girl, didn't he? A pity. She was a beauty."

My hand, which was holding a glass of port, tightened, the crystal groaning under the pressure. I did not move. I did not turn. If it were the old me, the first thing I would think of would be to defend, protect, and uphold his honor as an extension of my own honor. But that man was gone. That fragile alliance was a ruin. Now, I did not see a victim to be protected. I saw a puzzle to be solved, a potential conspirator whose secrets I needed to understand. I remained a statue of polite attention, my gaze fixed on the men I was supposed to be listening to, but my entire being was an instrument of eavesdropping, focused on the words being spoken behind me.

"Indeed," the first man continued, his voice dropping. "I heard he was still writing to her, even after the scandal broke. Utterly obsessed. Some say he never truly gave her up. A man like that, a romantic, doesn't just disappear. He lingers. A ghost at the feast, you might say."

The world seemed to tilt on its axis. My blood ran cold, and then hot, a wave of pure, unadulterated fury washing over me.

He lingers.

My mind, a cruel and efficient prosecutor, seized on the words. I saw it all with a sudden, devastating clarity. This was not a ghost. This was not a memory. This was an active, ongoing connection. My wife's secret sorrow, her retreat from me, her tormented, tear-filled nights—it was not for a man who was lost to her. It was for a man who was still a part of her life.

He was still writing to her.

The fragments of the conversation I had overheard between Marietta and her aunt now replayed in my mind, but this time they were not fragments. They were a complete, damning confession.

"...You lied to me... You told me I would never see him again... That he was gone forever."

It was not a memory of grief. It was an accusation of a present-day deception. Her family had not just lied to her about his death; they had been actively keeping her from him. And her aunt had thrown her at me, the Duke of Highmoor, as a solution. A way to chain her to a new life, to sever the ties with the old one.

I looked across the room at my wife. Lady Pembroke had moved on, leaving Marietta a solitary, pale figure on the settee. She was staring into the middle distance, her expression one of a profound, heartbreaking sadness. And I, in my blind, jealous rage, saw not the fragile Duchess exhausted by the cruelty of the *ton*. No, this was a deeper, more secret sorrow. I saw a woman grieving for a living lover she could not have.

The night we had shared at the inn, the passion I had believed was for me, now felt like a bitter, humiliating betrayal. Had she been thinking of him then? Had she closed her eyes and pretended I was another man? The thought was a vile, poisonous thing, a sickness that filled my soul.

The fragile, tentative hope I had nursed, the belief that we could build something real from the ashes of our arrangement, was not just broken. It was annihilated, reduced to dust by the casual, careless whispers of two old men.

I excused myself from the conversation with the backbenchers, my movements stiff, my face setting into the familiar, cold mask of ducal control. I began to walk toward her. The room was a cacophony of laughter and conversation, but for me, there was only silence and the sight of her, the

31

woman at the center of this intricate deception. I watched as she lifted a hand to her temple, a gesture of weariness I now reinterpreted as one of profound, secret pining. Every step I took toward her felt as if I were marching toward a battlefield.

I reached her side. She did not notice my approach until I spoke.

"Duchess," I said, my voice devoid of all warmth. "It is time to leave."

She looked up, startled, her eyes wide and unfocused for a fraction of a second before they registered my presence. I saw the fear leap into them as she took in my expression. It was the look of a hunted creature suddenly finding the predator standing over it. She rose without a word, a silent, obedient ghost, and placed her gloved hand on my offered arm. Her fingers trembled against my sleeve.

"Is Your Grace unwell?" she asked, her voice a strained whisper, already composing her features for the public performance of our exit.

"Merely weary of the company," I replied, my tone leaving no doubt as to where my displeasure lay.

We made our farewells, two perfect, smiling puppets on a string. I navigated us toward our hosts, my hand on her back, guiding her through the throng. I offered Lord Fitzgibbon a curt, flawless excuse regarding the Duchess's sudden fatigue. Marietta murmured her thanks, her voice a perfect, soft melody that belied the terror I knew she must feel from my coldness alone. We were magnificent liars.

The journey from the grand salon to the front door was a gauntlet of curious glances and deferential bows. My grip on her elbow tightened, a silent, possessive fury that she could not possibly have mistaken. I felt the slight tremor that ran through her, but she did not falter, her head held high, her smile fixed in place.

Only when the carriage door shut, sealing us into the intimate darkness, did the façade finally drop. She immediately pulled her hand from my arm and retreated to the furthest corner of the velvet squab, pressing herself against the side as if trying to merge with the shadows. The air in the carriage crackled with unspoken accusations.

The war between us was no longer silent. And as we rode through the dark streets of London, I would not rest until I had dragged every last one of her secrets into the light, no matter how much it destroyed us both.

6

The Storm in the Carriage

Callum

The journey home was a study in profound, hostile silence. The moment the carriage door shut, plunging us into the intimate darkness, the façade dropped. Marietta retreated to the furthest corner, a small, hunted animal, her face turned to the rain-streaked window, presenting me with nothing but the rigid, unforgiving line of her shoulder.

The air in the carriage crackled with my unspoken fury. Every word of the gossip I had overheard echoed in my mind, fueling a cold, burning rage. *He lingers. He was still writing to her.* I looked at my wife, this beautiful, sorrowful stranger, and I saw not a victim, but a conspirator in my own humiliation. The tenderness I had felt for her, the protective instinct, had curdled into a bitter, jealous poison.

I could not bear her silence. It felt like a judgment, a confirmation of her secret heart.

"Was that sadness for him, Marietta?" I asked, my voice a low, raw thing that cut through the rhythmic clatter of the wheels. "The ghost whose name is still whispered in every drawing room? Am I married to a memory? Am I to be nothing more than a name and a title to you, a convenience to shield you while your heart belongs to a ghost?"

She flinched as if struck, turning slowly from the window. Her face was pale in the flickering gaslight, her eyes wide with a mixture of shock and a pain that, for a moment, almost broke through my anger.

"You know nothing of my heart," she whispered, her voice trembling with a sudden, fierce passion. "You see ghosts where there are only shadows. Is this all I am to you? A scandal to be managed? A body to secure your line?"

Her accusation, the raw injustice of it after the genuine, aching tenderness I had begun to feel for her, shattered the last of my restraint. I moved across the carriage in a single, fluid motion, seating myself beside her, trapping her in the corner.

"You think that is all you are to me?" I growled, my face inches from hers. I could see the frantic pulse beating in her throat, smell the faint, clean scent of lavender on her skin. "You, who meet my eyes one moment with a fire that could burn down a city, and the next look away with a sorrow that does not belong to me? You are a riddle, a beautiful, maddening riddle. And I find I am no longer content to simply guess the answer."

I did not wait for her reply. I cupped her jaw, my thumb stroking the soft, trembling line of her lip, and then I kissed her. It was not a kiss of tenderness. It was a challenge, a question, an act of pure, frustrated passion.

For a single, heart-stopping second, she was rigid, her hands coming up to press against my chest in a gesture of resistance. And then, with a low, wounded sound, a sob that I swallowed with my own lips, she surrendered. She did not just melt; she answered. She kissed me back with a fervor that matched my own, a wild, desperate hunger that stole the air from my lungs. Her hands, which had been pushing me away, slid up my chest to tangle in my hair, pulling my head down, deepening the kiss until it was a raw, open-mouthed battle of tongues and teeth and breath.

The fire of our conflict transformed into a different kind of inferno. This was not a solution; it was an obliteration, a mutual, reckless surrender to the one force between us that was not a lie: this raw, undeniable, and desperate desire.

My hands were no longer content with her face. They slid down her throat, over the elegant line of her collarbone, to the bodice of her gown. My fingers

35

worked at the row of tiny buttons, my movements clumsy with an urgency that bordered on madness. She did not stop me. She aided me, her own trembling fingers fumbling with my cravat, pulling it loose, desperate to feel skin against skin.

The carriage rocked and swayed through the dark, wet streets of London, a small, private world hurtling through the night, and within it, we were creating a storm of our own. I pushed the heavy silk of her gown from her shoulders, my mouth following the path of my hands, tasting the cool, smooth skin. She cried out, a soft, broken sound, her head falling back against the velvet squab.

I pushed her chemise aside, freeing her breasts to my gaze. They were fuller, heavier than I remembered, the peaks already hard and flushed. A fresh wave of possessive fire shot through me. I took one in my mouth, suckling, my tongue laving the sensitive peak until she was a writhing, whimpering creature in my arms, her nails scoring my shoulders.

"Callum," she panted, the sound a desperate prayer.

The sound of my name on her lips, in this moment of raw, unguarded passion, was my undoing. I needed more. I needed all of her. I pushed her skirts up, my hand sliding up the smooth skin of her thigh. She gasped, her body arching against mine, a silent invitation. My fingers found the damp, secret heat of her, and she cried out, her hips moving against my hand in a frantic, beautiful rhythm.

She was ready. She was more than ready. She wanted this as much as I did.

I freed myself from the confines of my trousers, my own need a hard, aching thing. I positioned myself between her legs, the carriage swaying, creating a dizzying, intoxicating dance. "Look at me," I commanded, my voice a raw rasp.

She opened her eyes, and in their green, turbulent depths, I saw not fear, but a reflection of my own desperate, aching need.

I entered her then, a single, deep, and perfect thrust that joined us completely. She gasped, her body closing around me, a hot, wet glove of pure sensation. The rocking of the carriage, the feel of her beneath me, the scent of her skin—it was an assault on the senses, a beautiful, perfect madness.

I began to move, our bodies finding a rhythm that matched the frantic, swaying dance of the carriage. It was a rough, fast, and desperate coupling, a physical expression of all the anger and the longing that we could not put into words. Every thrust was a claim, every arch of her hips a surrender. But as she clung to me, her legs wrapped around my waist, a venomous whisper slithered into my mind. *Thorne.* The name was a shard of ice in the heart of our fire.

Had he known her like this? Had she cried out his name in a dusty, forgotten room while he took her?

A wild, jealous fury seized me. I was no longer making love to my wife; I was exorcising a ghost. I was branding her, marking her as mine in a way that would burn away the memory of any man who had come before. My thrusts became harder, deeper, punishing in their intensity. I was trying to drive his phantom from her body, from her soul.

She cried out, a sharp, high sound that was half pain, half pleasure. "Callum..."

The sound of my own name on her lips was not enough. I needed more. I leaned down, my mouth finding the sensitive skin of her neck, my teeth grazing her. "You are mine, Marietta," I growled against her, my voice a low, ragged thing. I drove into her again, faster now, a maddened, relentless rhythm. "Mine."

She didn't protest. She met my madness with her own, her hips rising to meet every sharp, punishing thrust. Her head thrashed on the velvet squab, her breath coming in short, sobbing gasps. "Yes... ah, yes..."

"Say my name," I commanded, my voice a hoarse whisper against her ear, needing to hear it again, needing it to be the only name she could think of, the only name she would ever cry out in passion again.

"Callum!" she screamed, the sound a beautiful, shattering thing. "Ah, Callum!"

That was it. That was my victory. The pleasure built, a relentless, rising tide, and at the sound of my name torn from her throat, I felt her body begin to convulse around me. I followed her over the edge, my own release a violent, shuddering wave, my own name a torn, ragged cry on her lips.

In the aftermath, we remained tangled together, our bodies slick with sweat, the scent of our passion thick in the small, enclosed space. I collapsed against her, my forehead resting on her shoulder, my breathing harsh in the sudden, profound silence.

I held her, her body a warm, pliant weight against mine, her head resting in the hollow of my shoulder. The silence that fell was not a hostile thing. It was a peaceful, sated quiet.

My hand, which had been gripping her hip, moved in a gesture of pure, sated instinct. I wanted to learn all of her, to possess every part of her. My hand slid up from the soft curve of her hip to rest on her belly, intending to trace idle patterns on the skin there. As my palm flattened against her, I registered something unexpected—not a curve, but a subtle, unfamiliar firmness low in her abdomen, a tautness beneath the soft skin that had not been there before.

She flinched.

It was not a large movement. It was a sudden, violent tightening of her muscles, a sharp, indrawn breath that was not of pleasure. Her entire body went rigid beneath me, her hands coming up to cover mine as if to push it away.

I froze, my hand hovering over her skin, the strange firmness I'd just felt forgotten, eclipsed by the raw terror in her reaction. The fire in my veins turned to ice. "Marietta?"

She did not answer. She squeezed her eyes shut, and in the dim light, I saw a look of pure, unadulterated terror on her face. A terror directed at my simple, innocent touch.

I withdrew my hand as if I had been burned and rolled off her, putting a foot of cold, empty space between us. The beautiful, fragile connection we had just forged was not just shattered; it was a lie.

My mind, a cold and logical engine, re-assessed the evidence. She had come to me willingly. She had met my passion with a fire that was fierce, genuine, and undeniable. And yet, the moment my hand touched her stomach, a place of simple, quiet intimacy, she had recoiled as if struck.

I saw it then, a truth more painful than any lie. Her body might desire me in a moment of reckless passion, but her soul, the core of her, belonged to another. That was the source of her illness. Her fatigue, her nausea, her pallor... they were not the symptoms of a delicate constitution. They were the symptoms of a secret, divided heart. The physical toll of a woman torn between the husband she was bound to and the lover she still secretly grieved for. She was not hiding an illness from me.

She was hiding her heart.

She had given me her body, yes. But the core of her, the center of her being, was a territory she would not allow me to touch. She had recoiled from me. The realization was a shard of ice in my gut. Our shared passion had not been a new beginning. It had been a temporary, physical solace from a deeper, emotional pain.

I looked at the woman beside me, now a stranger again, her face turned away, and I felt the cold, familiar armor of the Duke of Highmoor reassemble itself around my soul. I did not have her heart. But I had her body. And for now, in this fragile, stolen moment of peace, it would have to be enough.

7

The Silent Heartbeat

Marietta

The days following the Fitzgibbons' supper were a masterclass in the art of the fragile façade. Callum had retreated completely, his silence now laced with a new, cutting edge of suspicion. The air between us was thick with unspoken accusations, his every glance a silent interrogation. I did not know what had transpired to intensify his coldness, what new sin he had laid at my door, but I felt the shift in him as a palpable, chilling force. He was no longer just a distant, wounded man; he was my adversary, and the weight of his displeasure was a constant, heavy presence in our home.

I sought refuge, as I always did, in duty. I threw myself into the role of the Duchess with a feverish energy, my days a blur of household management, charitable committees, and the endless, exhausting performance of ducal life. It was a way to fill the silence, to outrun the ghosts that haunted my waking hours and the nightmares that plagued my sleep.

It was this relentless pursuit of normalcy that led me, one stiflingly warm afternoon, to the establishment of Madame Dubois, the city's most sought-after and discreet modiste. The upcoming season demanded new gowns, and the Duchess of Highmoor was expected to be a paragon of fashion. It was a tedious, necessary errand, another line in the play I was performing.

The shop was a jewel box of silks and velvets, the air thick with the scent of French perfume and hot irons. Madame Dubois herself, a small, bird-like woman with eyes as sharp as her needles, fussed around me, her French accent a torrent of flattering superlatives.

"For Your Grace, for the Lansdowne ball, I envision a celestial blue," she chirped, unfurling a bolt of silk that shimmered like a captured piece of the evening sky. "Simple, elegant, with a whisper of silver thread at the hem. It will be perfection."

"That sounds lovely, Madame," I murmured, trying to summon a flicker of interest I did not feel.

I was led to the fitting room, a small, airless chamber at the back of the shop, its walls lined with mirrors that reflected my pale, weary face back at me from a dozen different angles. A young seamstress, her mouth a bristle of pins, helped me out of my day dress and into the stiff, unforgiving corset that was the necessary foundation of our fashion.

She began to pull the laces. "Tighter, Your Grace?" she asked, her voice muffled.

"Yes, please, Anna," I said, my voice a little breathless as the stays began to bite into my ribs. The familiar, caging pressure was a comfort in its own way, a physical manifestation of the emotional constraints that defined my life.

But today, it felt different. The pressure was not just containing; it was suffocating. As she pulled the laces taut, a wave of dizziness, faint at first, then more pronounced, washed over me. The reflection in the mirror wavered, the dozen Mariettas swimming in and out of focus.

"Perhaps that is sufficient," I managed to say, placing a hand on the wall to steady myself.

The seamstress, oblivious, gave one final, expert tug. "Perfection, Your Grace."

She and Madame Dubois then began to drape the celestial blue silk over me, their hands quick and impersonal, their voices a low, professional murmur as they discussed darts and seams and the precise placement of a satin rosette.

The room was growing warmer, the air thick and heavy. The scent of the silk, of the women's perfume, of the hot iron from the next room, all seemed to coalesce into a cloying, oppressive cloud.

A high, thin ringing began in my ears. The women's voices seemed to recede, becoming a distant, meaningless buzz. The edges of my vision began to darken, the bright, cluttered room narrowing into a small, wavering tunnel of light.

"Your Grace?" Madame Dubois's voice cut through the fog, sharp with a sudden alarm. "You are as pale as a sheet. Anna, a glass of water!"

I tried to respond, to assure them I was fine, but my tongue felt thick and useless in my mouth. I saw the seamstress's eyes widen in horror as she looked at my face. I felt my own eyes roll back in my head, a sensation of falling from a great height, and then the world dissolved into a soft, welcoming darkness.

I came to with a gasp, the scent of lavender water sharp in my nostrils. I was no longer in the fitting room. I was lying on a plush velvet chaise in a small, quiet back room, a cool, damp cloth resting on my forehead. The tight, suffocating corset was gone, the laces of my chemise loosened. Sunlight streamed through a single, grimy window, illuminating dancing dust motes in the air.

For a moment, I was utterly disoriented. And then, the memory of my collapse came rushing back, bringing with it a wave of hot, profound humiliation. I, the Duchess of Highmoor, had fainted in a dressmaker's shop like some sentimental, weak-willed heroine from a novel. The gossip would be all over town by nightfall.

A man cleared his throat, a quiet, discreet sound. I turned my head. A gentleman, his hair grey at the temples, a black medical bag at his feet, was sitting in a chair beside the chaise. Through the closed door, I could hear the faint, hushed murmur of voices—Madame Dubois's calm, authoritative French, and the higher, more frantic tones of my maid, Anna. They were being kept outside. We were entirely alone.

He was holding my wrist, his fingers pressed gently against my pulse point. He was not a society physician I recognized. He was older, his face kind but serious, his clothes respectable but not fashionable. He was the very picture of quiet, professional discretion. Madame Dubois, I realized, was a woman who knew how to handle a crisis without inviting a scandal.

"The heat... I'm just a bit lightheaded," I insisted weakly, attempting to sit up. The movement sent a fresh wave of dizziness through me, and I sank back against the cushions with a low groan.

The doctor gently urged me to remain reclining. "A momentary weakness, Your Grace," he said, his voice a low, calming murmur. "Quite understand-able, under the circumstances." He released my wrist and his gaze, kind but clinical, dropped for a fraction of a second to my abdomen.

My heart, which had been beating a slow, sluggish rhythm, gave a single, violent thud against my ribs. A cold, prickling dread washed over me.

"The circumstances?" I whispered, my voice a thin, reedy thing.

The doctor leaned forward slightly, his voice dropping so low it was barely audible, a sound meant only for my ears, a sound that would not carry past the closed door where my maid waited.

"Your Grace," he said, his expression softening with a gentle, almost paternal kindness, "you are with child."

The world stopped. The motes of dust ceased their dance. The distant sounds of the street outside faded to nothing. There was only the quiet, sunlit room and the doctor's words, which seemed to hang in the air like a physical presence.

With child.

My heart, which had just stopped, now began to pound, a wild, frantic, terrified rhythm. Pregnant. My hand, as if with a will of its own, drifted down to my still-flat stomach, my fingers spreading over the place where a new life, a secret life, had taken root.

A storm of emotion, so violent and so contradictory it threatened to tear me apart, crashed over me. There was a surge of pure, unadulterated joy, a radiant, incandescent bliss so powerful it brought tears to my eyes. A child. A baby. Callum's child. After all the loneliness, all the pain, I had been given this. A new life. A new hope. A chance, however fragile, to build the family I had been so brutally denied. The longing I had felt at Ravenswood, the aching, maternal need that had been reawakened by Isabelle, had been answered.

But hot on the heels of that joy came a wave of terror so cold and so absolute it threatened to extinguish the fragile flame of my happiness. A child. Now. In the midst of this cold war, with a husband who looked at me with suspicion and contempt. How could I tell him? How could I announce this miraculous, beautiful news into the frozen wasteland of our marriage?

I thought of his face when he had spoken of his first wife, of the raw, bitter pain of her betrayal. I thought of his suspicion of me, his belief that my heart belonged to another. To tell him now that I was with child... he would not see it as a blessing. In his current state of mind, he would see it as a trap. A complication. Perhaps even, in his darkest, most cynical moments, as another woman's lie. The thought was a physical pain, a blade twisting in my gut.

And then there was Isabelle. My secret. My firstborn. To announce this new pregnancy would be to invite a new level of scrutiny into my life, into my health, into my past. It would be to celebrate a new child while my first remained a ghost, a secret I was forced to carry in silence. The hypocrisy of it, the profound, tragic injustice, was a fresh wave of grief.

Remembering how gossip spreads, how fragile my situation with Callum was, I knew I could not reveal this. Not yet. Revealing my pregnancy now could push his fragile emotions over the edge, invite society's scrutiny while I was still guarding Isabelle's secret, and perhaps even endanger the fragile life that was just beginning within me.

The physician, accustomed to the delicate and often secret troubles of the nobility, seemed to read the storm of terror and conflict on my face.

"Doctor," I whispered, my voice trembling as I struggled to sit up. "How... how long?"

He gently pressed on my shoulder, urging me to remain reclining. "It is difficult to be precise, Your Grace, but based on my examination, I would estimate you are between six and eight weeks along. The slight hardening of the uterus is quite normal for this stage, so you must not be alarmed by it. Everything, for now, appears to be as it should."

His clinical, reassuring words were a strange comfort, a small, solid fact in a world that had just dissolved into chaos. Six to eight weeks. The timing was undeniable. It was the result of that one, desperate, passionate night at the inn on our way back from Ravenswood. The memory of it, of the warmth and hope I had felt, was a stark and painful contrast to the cold reality of my current situation.

I reached out, my fingers closing weakly around the sleeve of his coat. "Doctor, please," I whispered, my voice a raw, desperate plea. "No one can know of this. Not yet. Not even... not even the Duke. I beg of you, your word of honor."

He paused, his kind eyes taking in my panicked expression with a look of profound, gentle understanding. He placed his free hand over mine in a comforting, paternal gesture.

"Your Grace," he said gently, his voice a low murmur. "You may rest assured of my complete discretion. Madame Dubois is a trusted friend. Nothing of what has passed in this room will ever leave it. You have my word."

He understood. He did not know my reasons, but he understood my need for silence. I gave him a weak, grateful nod, unable to speak past the lump of tears and fear in my throat.

He gave me a few simple instructions—to rest, to avoid tight corsets, to send for him if the faintness returned—and then he was gone, leaving me alone with my new, beautiful, and terrifying secret.

A short time later, cloaked and veiled, I left the shop through a discreet back entrance, a silent, shadowy figure slipping back into the bright, unforgiving light of London. My mind was a whirlwind. I carried Callum's heir, a precious, impossible hope for our marriage, a silent heartbeat that might, one day, bridge the chasm between us. But for now, it was also a new and terrible burden of secrecy.

The cracks in the fragile façade of my life were spreading, threatening to shatter the entire, delicate structure. And as the carriage carried me back to the cold, silent grandeur of Redwyck House, I clutched my hand over my abdomen and prayed. I prayed that the cracks would hold, just a little longer, until I found the right time, the right way, to tell my husband the truth. About everything.

8

A Secret Kept

Marietta

The journey back to Redwyck House was a blur. I sat rigid in the corner of the carriage, the veiled hat pulled low, my hands clenched tightly in my lap. The sounds of London—the rattle of wheels on cobblestones, the calls of street vendors, the distant chime of a church bell— were a muted, meaningless drone. My entire world had contracted to the space within my own body, to the silent, secret heartbeat that had just been given a name.

You are with child.

The doctor's words echoed in my mind, a mantra of joy and of terror. I was a tempest of conflicting emotions, a sea tossed between the ecstatic shores of hope and the jagged, deadly rocks of my own fear. I carried my husband's heir. A precious, impossible gift. A fragile hope for a future I had never dared to imagine. And it was a secret I now had to guard with my very life.

The moment I stepped into the grand, silent hall of the house, the weight of my performance settled back onto my shoulders. The footman who took my cloak saw nothing but his Duchess, returned from an afternoon of shopping, her expression perhaps a little weary from the endeavor. He did not see the woman whose entire world had just been irrevocably altered, the mother who was now carrying two secrets so monumental they threatened to crush her.

I made my way to my chambers, my steps slow and deliberate, a perfect picture of ducal grace. But the moment the heavy oak door closed behind me, sealing me into the solitude of my rooms, the façade crumbled.

"Anna," I said, my voice a tight, breathless thing. My maid, who had been tidying my dressing table, turned, her expression one of polite inquiry. "Please... help me with this dress. It is insufferably warm."

"Of course, Your Grace," she murmured, her fingers moving to the row of tiny buttons at my back.

I stood as still as a statue as she worked, my mind a chaotic whirlwind. With every button that was undone, with every layer that was peeled away, I felt not a release, but a new, more profound sense of being trapped. The dress was a cage, but my own body, my own secrets, were a prison far more absolute.

When I was finally down to my chemise, I turned to her. "Thank you, Anna. You may leave me. I... I have a slight headache. I wish to lie down for a while. See that I am not disturbed."

"Very good, Your Grace," she said with a small curtsy, and then she was gone, leaving me in the quiet, sunlit stillness of my own chamber.

I was alone. Truly alone with my secret.

I did not go to the settee. I went to the bed, the vast, lonely expanse of it, and I lay down on my back, the cool linen a shock against my heated skin. The room was silent save for the soft ticking of the clock on the mantelpiece, each tick a second of my new, secret life passing by.

Slowly, as if in a trance, my hand moved to my stomach. It was still flat, the fine lawn of my chemise lying smooth over my skin. There was no outward sign, no visible proof of the miracle that was unfolding within me. But I knew.

I closed my eyes, and my mind was immediately pulled back four years, to another room, another life. I remembered the first, secret months of my pregnancy with Isabelle. I remembered lying just like this, in a strange, lonely bed in Northumberland, my hand spread over my own belly, feeling the first, subtle changes. I remembered the almost imperceptible rounding, a secret known only to me. Then, the gradual, miraculous swell as she grew, my stomach transforming from a soft curve into a firm, proud globe. I remembered the first, fluttering kick, a sensation like the wings of a trapped butterfly, a secret language between a mother and her unborn child.

My fingers traced the skin of my abdomen now, an unconscious, searching gesture. The doctor had said my uterus was hardening, a normal sign. I pressed gently, and for a fraction of a second, I thought I could feel it, a subtle, deep firmness that was not there before. Or perhaps it was only my imagination, my memory superimposing itself upon the present.

Tears pricked my eyes, hot and sharp. Then, I had been alone, terrified of the shame, but filled with a fierce, uncomplicated love for the child I carried. Now, I was a Duchess, a wife, and my joy was poisoned by a fear that was a thousand times more complex.

How long? The question was a frantic whisper in my mind. How long did I have?

The doctor had said six to eight weeks. I counted on my fingers, my mind a frantic calculator. A month, perhaps two at the most, with the clever draping of Madame Dubois's designs, and then the gentle swell would become undeniable. By then, the secret would be impossible to hide. I had a handful of weeks, nothing more.

And what of the nights? My heart hammered at the thought. Our physical relations, however emotionally distant, were a ducal duty Callum had shown no intention of forsaking. How long could I possibly hide such a secret from a husband who shared my bed? How long before his hands, moving over me in the darkness, noticed the new fullness of my breasts, or the subtle, unfamiliar firmness low in my abdomen? To deny him would be to sound an alarm, to invite a suspicion far more dangerous than any I had yet faced. But to allow him close was to risk discovery with every touch. The thought of him discovering it before I was ready, of him looking at me with that cool, analytical assessment as my body changed, was a new and specific terror.

It wasn't that I didn't want to be honest. My God, I ached to be. I ached to go to him now, to take his hand and place it on my stomach, to share this miraculous, terrifying joy with him. But the trauma of my first pregnancy was a ghost that still held me in its cold grip. I remembered my father's face, the disgust, the cold fury. I remembered his words—*disgrace, stain, a problem to be erased.*

Would Callum be any different? He was a man of honor, yes. But he was also a Duke, a man whose entire life was built on a foundation of lineage, of propriety, of an absolute intolerance for scandal. And I was married to him under a false pretense. He did not know the full, ugly truth of my ruin. To tell him now, to confess not just this new life, but the secret of the old one... I could not predict his reaction. I could not risk seeing that warmth I had glimpsed in his eyes turn to the same cold disgust I had seen in my father's.

A sharp, authoritative knock on the door shattered the quiet of the room. I started, my eyes flying open, my hand dropping from my stomach as if I had been burned.

"Enter," I called, my voice a breathy, panicked thing as I scrambled to sit up, pulling a silken robe around my shoulders to hide the state of my undress.

The door opened, and Callum stood on the threshold. He was still in his day clothes, a folio of papers in his hand. He stopped, his eyes widening in surprise as he took in the scene—me, half-dressed, sitting on the edge of my bed in the middle of the afternoon.

"Marietta?" he said, a frown creasing his brow. "Are you unwell?"

"No," I said, the lie coming too quickly, too breathlessly. I rose to my feet, clutching the robe tightly around me. "Forgive my appearance. The day was... warm. I was merely resting."

He walked further into the room, his gaze sweeping over me, a familiar, analytical look in his eyes that made my skin prickle. "I received a note from Madame Dubois's assistant," he said, his voice the cool, formal instrument of the Duke. "She informed me you were taken ill at the shop. That you fainted."

My blood ran cold. Of course. An event involving the Duchess would be reported to the Duke immediately. He was not just my husband; he was the man who noticed everything, the man whose suspicion was a constant, low-grade hum in our lives.

"It was nothing," I insisted, my hand unconsciously coming up to rest on my abdomen as I spoke, a desperate, protective gesture. "The room was stuffy, the corset too tight. A momentary weakness, that is all." I quickly dropped my hand as I realized what I was doing. "As for why I did not purchase a gown," I continued, moving towards my dressing table to turn my back to him, desperate to escape his penetrating gaze, "She has some lovely new silks from Lyon. I asked her to send the catalog here. I found I could not make a decision in the shop."

It was a plausible excuse, the action of a discerning, indecisive Duchess. I prayed he would accept it, that he had not seen my small, betraying gesture. I heard him pause behind me, and I held my breath, waiting for the next question, the next probe. But it did not come.

"Very well," he said finally, his voice a flat, unreadable thing. "See that you do not over-exert yourself. You have been looking... tired lately."

"I shall, Your Grace," I murmured, my gaze dropping to the floor in a perfect imitation of wifely deference. "You are most considerate. I will be sure to rest."

And then he was gone, the door closing with a soft, final click behind him. I was left alone, my reflection a pale, haunted stranger in the mirror. I had survived. I had kept the secret. For now. But as I stared at my own wide, terrified eyes, I knew, with a chilling certainty, that I was not just hiding a child. I was building a wall, brick by secret brick, between myself and my husband, a wall that I was beginning to fear might soon become too high for either of us to ever climb.

9

A Joyful Terror

Marietta

The week that followed the doctor's diagnosis was a strange, secret purgatory of joy and terror. I lived a double life, not just in public, but within the confines of my own skin. My body was no longer entirely my own; it was the sacred, secret vessel of a new life, a new hope. And my mind was a battlefield, a constant, warring landscape of elation and dread.

In the quiet, solitary moments, when I was alone in my chambers with no performance to give, the joy was a thing so pure and so potent it was almost a physical pain. I would stand before the tall pier glass, my hands spread protectively over my still-flat abdomen, and I would whisper to the tiny, secret life within.

A baby. My baby. Callum's baby.

The words were a prayer, a mantra of disbelief and of wonder. After all the loss, all the grief, and the aching loneliness of a mother separated from her child, I had been given another. The irony was a cruel and beautiful thing. A child conceived not in a reckless, youthful folly, but in a storm of raw, undeniable passion with the man who was my husband. A child who would be a Redwyck, an heir, a legitimate and cherished soul from the very first beat of its tiny heart—a child I would be allowed to keep. The thought was a blessing so profound it brought me to my knees, yet it felt like a fresh betrayal of the daughter I still could not claim.

Tears would stream down my face in these secret moments, but they were not the hot, bitter tears of grief I had grown so accustomed to. They were tears of a gratitude so profound it felt like a holy thing. I thought of the future, a future I had never dared to imagine. I saw a nursery, not the one at Ravenswood that I could only visit as a stranger, but one here, in this house, filled with light and laughter. I saw Callum, not as the Duke of Ice, but as a father, his stern face softened with a love I now knew he was capable of. I saw a family. Our family. The hope of it was a radiant, painful light that seemed to fill the cold, empty spaces of my heart.

But as the week bled into the next, my secret began to take on a physical form. The abdomen that had been flat was no longer so. Each morning, I would stand before the pier glass after my bath, my heart hammering, and I would see it—a slight, undeniable curve that had not been there the day before. To me, it was as prominent as a banner, a declaration of my duplicity. I felt like a criminal, my body the evidence of a crime I was desperately trying to conceal. Every rustle of silk, every pull of a corset lace, brought a fresh wave of panic. Did my maid notice how she had to let out the seams of my morning gown? Did Callum's cool, analytical gaze linger for a fraction of a second too long on my waistline as we sat at dinner? I felt exposed, caught red-handed in a truth my own body was beginning to tell, and the constant fear of discovery was a torment.

This joy, therefore, was a fragile, secret treasure, a candle flame I had to shield with my entire being from the cold, hostile winds of my reality. The moment I stepped out of my chambers, the joy was forced to retreat, replaced by a constant, humming anxiety, a fear so pervasive it was like a second skin.

The terror had a thousand faces.

First, and most immediate, was the fear of Callum. My husband. The father of my child. He should have been the first person I ran to, the one with whom I shared this miraculous news. But the man who had returned from Ravenswood was a stranger, a cold, watchful adversary. To tell him now, in the midst of this icy war, felt impossible. His suspicion was a tangible thing in every room we shared. How could I announce a pregnancy into that poisoned atmosphere? He would not see a blessing. He would see a complication, a trap, another secret I had kept from him.

His first wife's betrayal was a ghost that haunted every corner of our marriage. I knew, with a certainty that chilled me to the bone, that any hint of a secret, especially one concerning a child, would touch upon his deepest, most painful wound. I had seen the flash of suspicion in his eyes when his aunt had first suggested the possibility. My desperate, risky bluff with the doctor had quelled it, for now. But to announce it myself, after weeks of silent suffering and strange symptoms... he would question everything. The timing. My motives. My honesty.

The fragile, tentative trust we had begun to build would be annihilated. He would see me not as his wife, but as his enemy, a schemer who had once again hidden a truth of monumental importance from him. And the thought of seeing that cold, wounded disgust in his eyes again was a pain I did not think I could bear.

And so, I began to hide. The act of concealing my own child from its father was a profound, daily betrayal that ate at my soul, but I saw no other choice. It was a temporary measure, I told myself, a necessary deception until the frost between us thawed, until I could find a moment of peace, a flicker of the old warmth, in which to tell him the truth.

My life became a masterpiece of subtle evasion. My wardrobe, once a source of ducal pride, was now a strategic arsenal. I instructed my maid to bring forward gowns from earlier in the season, gowns with looser waistlines, with clever draping and jackets that would conceal the very subtle changes in my figure that I was sure were only visible to my own panicked eyes. I would plead a chill in the air to wear a shawl, even on a warm afternoon. Every morning was a careful calculation, a choice of fabrics and styles designed to obscure, to deflect, to lie.

Dinners became a new form of torture. The nausea was a constant, unwelcome companion, a physical manifestation of my own inner turmoil. The rich, fragrant sauces, the roasted meats, the very scent of the wine he drank, would turn my stomach. I became an expert at moving food around on my plate, at taking tiny, bird-like bites, at raising my napkin to my lips to hide a sudden wave of queasiness.

The deception, however, could not be contained forever. One evening, as I was preparing for bed, a sharp knock came at my door. It was Callum. He entered without waiting for my reply, his face a mask of grim concern.

"Mrs. Finch has informed me that you have been... unwell," he said, his voice flat. "She tells me you have been sick in the mornings for the past week."

My blood ran cold. The staff was watching. Reporting. I was a prisoner under constant surveillance. I clutched the lapels of my robe, my hand instinctively coming to rest over the gentle but undeniable curve of my abdomen.

"It is nothing, Your Grace," I lied, forcing a weary sigh. "A mere acute indigestion. The stress of our return to London... it has unsettled my nerves, that is all."

He made a small, sharp sound, a cynical click of his tongue against his teeth that was more dismissive than any shout. His gaze flickered to my hand on my stomach, and a look of profound, bitter understanding crossed his features. He believed he knew the source of my "stress," and it had nothing to do with London. It had to do with a ghost named Thorne.

I watched him across the vast expanse of the table, my heart aching with the weight of my secret. I wanted to share this with him. I wanted to see the joy, the shock, the hope in his eyes. I wanted to place his hand on my stomach and have him feel the miracle we had created. But all he saw was a pale, distant wife whose secret grief for another man was making her physically ill, a woman who was retreating further and further away from him. My necessary secrecy was, I knew, only fueling his suspicion, widening the chasm between us. I was trying to protect our future, but I was destroying our present.

Then there was the fear for Isabelle. My daughter. My firstborn. My other, more established, secret. The thought of a new baby, of a legitimate Redwyck heir, filled me with a joy that was immediately poisoned by a sharp, cutting guilt. How could I celebrate this new life when my first was still a secret, a ghost in my own history? It felt like a betrayal of her, a denial of her very existence.

And what would happen when this new child was born? The presence of a ducal heir would change everything. The focus of the family, of the world, would be on the nursery at Redwyck House. Would Isabelle be forgotten? Would she become a less-cherished relation, a ward to be raised in the country while her... half sibling... was raised in the heart of society? The thought of her being pushed aside, of her feeling in any way less loved, was a fresh torment.

I was living in a state of joyful terror, my heart pulled in a thousand different directions. I was a mother to two children, one a secret from the world, the other a secret from her own father. I was a wife to a man I was beginning to love, a man I was profoundly deceiving. I was the Duchess of Highmoor, a woman of grace and poise, and I was Marietta Greystone, a woman on the verge of shattering completely.

I prayed. In the silent darkness of my room, I would clutch the small, worn bootie I kept hidden in my jewelry box, the only tangible piece of Isabelle's infancy, and I would pray for guidance, for strength, for a path through this impossible labyrinth. I prayed for a miracle, for a moment of grace that would allow me to reveal the truth without destroying everything I held dear.

But no miracle came. There was only the slow, inexorable passage of time, the silent, secret growth of the new life within me, and the ever-widening distance between myself and my husband. The cracks in the fragile façade of my life were spreading, and I knew, with a cold, hollow certainty, that it was only a matter of time before it all came crashing down.

10

A Dangerous Proximity

Marietta

The news arrived, as most pronouncements in this house did, through a servant. It was late afternoon, and I was sitting by the window in my chambers, a book lying unread in my lap. My thoughts were a tangled knot of love for one child and fear for another.

But as the days since the doctor's visit had bled into a week, and then another, my secret had begun to take on a physical form. The abdomen that had been flat was no longer so. The change was subtle, but to my own panicked eyes, it was a declaration. Each morning, I would stand before the pier glass after my bath, my heart hammering, and I would see it—a slight, undeniable curve that had not been there before. I felt like a criminal, my body the evidence of a crime I was desperately trying to conceal. Every rustle of silk, every pull of a corset lace, brought a fresh wave of panic. I felt exposed, caught red-handed in a truth my own body was beginning to tell.

My maid, Anna, entered after a soft knock.

"Your Grace," she said, her eyes respectfully downcast. "His Grace sends his compliments and informs you that he will be joining you in your chambers this evening after he has finished with his dispatches."

The air rushed from my lungs. My hand flew to my stomach, a gesture of pure, maternal instinct. In the week that had passed since our wild, desperate encounter in the carriage, a new and confounding distance had settled between us. He had thrown himself into his duties with a fervor, spending his days with his steward and his nights in his study, often not returning to his own wing until the early hours of the morning. Our nights, after that one, brief conflagration, had once again become a cold and lonely truce. He had not sought my bed again, and I, consumed by my own secrets, had not dared to seek his. But now... now he was coming. The fragile, uncertain peace was over.

"Thank you, Anna," I managed to say, my voice steady despite the frantic hammering of my heart. "Please, see that a bath is drawn. And lay out the ivory silk nightgown."

"At once, Your Grace," the maid murmured, giving a small curtsy before moving silently to the adjoining bathing chamber.

As Anna bustled about, the distant sound of running water a prelude to the evening's ordeal, I remained by the window, my hand still pressed against the slight, firm curve of my abdomen. The terror was a cold, sharp thing. How was I to hide this? How was I to endure the scrutiny of his touch, the intimacy of his embrace, without my body betraying the secret it held? To deny him would invite a suspicion more dangerous than any I had yet faced. I had no choice but to proceed, to walk the thinnest of tightropes over a chasm of ruin.

Later, as I soaked in the hot, scented water of the bath, I found myself unconsciously rubbing my stomach. The skin felt tender, the muscles beneath tight and unfamiliar.

"Is Your Grace feeling unwell?" Anna asked from beside the tub, her voice laced with a genuine, simple concern that was a small knife in my heart.

I forced a casual, dismissive laugh. "It is nothing, Anna," I lied, the excuse coming easily to my lips. "A woman's complaint. My monthly courses are due, and my stomach feels... unsettled. It is of no consequence."

She accepted the explanation without question, her duty fulfilled. But I knew the lie was a temporary shield, a fragile defense against a far more intimate examination to come.

Dressed in the ivory silk, my hair brushed until it shone in the candlelight,

I waited. I was a sacrifice being prepared for the altar, my body a vessel of secrets, my mind a storm of fear and a strange, traitorous anticipation. When his knock finally came, firm and authoritative, my heart leaped into my throat.

He entered, a formidable figure in a dark silk dressing gown, the scent of brandy and clean linen preceding him. He said nothing. He simply walked to me, his grey eyes dark and unreadable in the dim light, and lowered his head to kiss me.

The kiss was not angry, not desperate, but a slow, claiming heat that spoke of a deep and undeniable need. I responded, my mind screaming warnings while my body, that willing traitor, melted against him. His mouth left mine to trail a path of fire down my throat, his lips and tongue a delicious torment against my sensitive skin.

He pushed the thin silk straps of my gown from my shoulders, his hands warm and sure on my skin. His kisses moved lower, over my collarbone, to the swell of my breasts. My head fell back, a silent surrender to the sheer, overwhelming pleasure of his touch.

And then his mouth was on my stomach.

He licked a slow, wet path from my navel downwards, his tongue a brand against my skin. I gasped, my fingers tangling in his hair. He paused, his lips still against me, and I felt him frown. His hand came to rest where his mouth had been, his palm flattening against my lower abdomen. He rubbed the area, his touch no longer a caress, but a questioning, analytical exploration.

"You feel... different," he murmured against my skin, his voice a low, curious rumble. "Firm."

Panic, cold and absolute, shot through me. He had noticed. I had to distract him, now, before his sharp, intelligent mind could begin to piece the puzzle together. I threaded my fingers through his hair and pulled his head up, capturing his mouth with my own in a deep, demanding kiss, pouring all of my fear and my desperation into the act. I moved against him, a silent, desperate plea for him to forget his curiosity and lose himself in the passion of the moment.

For a moment, I thought it had worked. He groaned into my mouth, his own desire reigniting. His fingers left my stomach and slid lower, tangling in the dark curls at the juncture of my thighs. He found the slick, wet heat of me, and my body betrayed me with a sharp, involuntary arch of my hips. I tried not to react, to remain a passive recipient, but his touch was a devastatingly skillful thing, and a whimper of pure pleasure escaped my lips.

He moved over me then, his intention clear. He meant to lie on top of me, his heavy, masculine weight pressing me into the soft mattress. And a new wave of terror, this one purely maternal, crashed over me. The baby. My hand flew to his chest, not to push him away, but to stop him.

"No," I whispered, my voice a ragged, breathless thing.

I saw the flash of anger and wounded pride in his eyes, the familiar, cold look that I so dreaded. But before he could speak, before the misunderstanding could take root, I acted.

"Let me," I said, my voice dropping to a husky, seductive whisper I barely recognized as my own. I pushed gently against his shoulders, reversing our positions until I was the one kneeling over him, my hair a dark curtain around us. I was on top, in control, my belly safe from any crushing weight.

The anger in his eyes was replaced by a look of dark, surprised pleasure. He did not seem suspicious at all. He seemed... delighted. A low, appreciative chuckle rumbled in his chest as he settled back against the pillows, his hands coming up to grip my hips, his touch a possessive, inviting heat. "By all means, Duchess," he murmured. "Lead the way."

My heart hammered against my ribs, a frantic rhythm of fear and a wild, traitorous excitement. I had taken control out of a desperate, maternal instinct to protect my child, but now I was faced with the terrifying, exhilarating consequence. His hard length pressed against me, a promise of the pleasure and the danger to come.

With my hands braced on the hard planes of his chest, I rose up slightly on my knees, the ivory silk of my nightgown pooling around my thighs. He watched me through hooded, hungry eyes, his hands a steady, guiding presence on my hips. For a long, breathless moment, I hesitated, suspended above him in the flickering firelight. Then, taking a shuddering breath that was half-sob, half-surrender, I lowered myself onto him.

The feeling of him entering me was a slow, deliberate fire, a stretching, filling sensation that stole the air from my lungs. I gasped, my head falling back as my body accepted all of him, sheathing him in my own wet heat. He groaned, a low, guttural sound of pure pleasure, his fingers digging into the soft flesh of my hips as I took him completely.

At first, my movements were slow, tentative, a cautious exploration. But his hands on me were a silent, firm command, guiding my rhythm, encouraging me. He began to thrust up to meet me, a powerful, steady rhythm that sent shudders of pure sensation through me. The dance became faster, fiercer, a desperate, beautiful battle. It was a clash of secrets and desires, his powerful thrusts meeting the frantic, searching movements of my own hips.

The pleasure was a rising tide, a merciless, exquisite storm that threatened to shatter my carefully constructed composure. With every upward thrust of his hips, a whimper escaped my lips. I was losing myself, my control, my very sense of self. And in that loss, the fear returned, a cold counterpoint to the heat in my veins. This felt too real, too intimate. He would know. In the throes of this pleasure, my body would betray me, would tell him the secrets my lips could not.

The thought sent a fresh jolt of panicked energy through me, pushing me faster, harder, as if I could outrun the truth itself. I felt the climax building, a tight, coiling knot of sensation deep within me. I cried out, a high, keening sound, my back arching as the first wave crashed over me. I shuddered violently, my body convulsing around him, clinging to him as the pleasure tore through me, so intense it was indistinguishable from pain.

My release triggered his. With a final, powerful thrust, he stiffened, a raw, guttural groan tearing from his throat. The force of it all, the storm of sensation and emotion, was too much. My strength gave out completely. I collapsed forward, a dead weight, my body boneless and spent.

I did not hit the mattress. Strong arms wrapped around me instantly, catching me, pulling me tight against a sweat-slick chest. He held me, his own body still trembling with the aftershocks of his release, his heart hammering against my ear. His arms were a cage of iron and warmth, holding the shattered pieces of me together.

Our lovemaking had ended. We had found a shared, shattering release in each other's arms, our cries mingling in the firelit darkness. But as he held me, his breathing slowly returning to normal, I knew, with a familiar, aching certainty, that nothing had been solved.

Afterward, he did not leave. He pulled me down beside him, his arm a secure, possessive weight around me, and drew me against his chest. Within minutes, the steady, even rhythm of his breathing told me he was asleep.

I lay there in the dark, listening to the soft, gentle sound of his snores, my heart a painful, aching knot in my chest. He was so close, yet the chasm between us was a universe wide.

Slowly, carefully, my own hand moved, capturing his where it rested on my waist. I lifted it, his fingers limp and warm in mine, and I gently, reverently, placed his hand on my stomach. I held it there, my own hand covering his, a silent, secret communion.

He did not know. And I could not tell him, not yet. But the child within me, our child, deserved to feel its father's touch, even if it was only in sleep. And for a few, precious, stolen moments in the dark, we were a family. The three of us. United in a truth that only two of us could feel, and only one of us knew.

11

An Unspoken Suspicion

Callum

The house was quieter than it had ever been. It was a silence of a different, more insidious quality than the hostile void that had defined the first weeks of our marriage. Before, the silence had been an empty battlefield between us. Now, it was a fog, a thick, muffling blanket of my wife's own making, and I was lost within it, my frustration growing with every passing, impenetrable day.

I had been a fool. In the raw, emotional aftermath of our argument, in the fire of a passion I had mistaken for a shared, desperate need, I had believed we had found a new, more honest language. I had believed that the physical act had been a brutal but necessary catharsis, a storm that would clear the air. Instead, it had become another secret she kept from me, another locked room in the sprawling, haunted manor of her heart.

She was a ghost in my house. A pale, beautiful specter who drifted through the grand rooms, her smile a fragile, paper-thin thing, her eyes shadowed with a grief I was beginning to believe was an impassable chasm between us. I watched her. I, who was accustomed to solving the most complex political intrigues, found myself utterly confounded by the woman who bore my name. I studied her across the dinner table, at public functions, in the rare moments

I caught her gaze in the hallway, and I saw a woman who was slowly, quietly, disintegrating.

The changes were subtle at first, small cracks in the perfect, serene façade she presented to the world. I first noticed the fatigue. She had always possessed a quiet, dignified stillness, but this was different. This was a profound, bone-deep weariness. I would find her in the afternoon drawing room, a book open but unread in her lap, her head resting against the back of the settee, her eyes closed. She was not sleeping, merely... absent. As if the sheer effort of existing, of breathing the same air as the rest of the world, had become too much for her.

At social functions, I would see the energy drain from her halfway through the evening. Her smiles would become a little more strained, her posture a little less perfect. She would find a quiet corner, a chair behind a potted palm, and retreat into herself, a solitary island in a sea of glittering society. I knew the gossips saw it. They saw the Duchess of Highmoor, looking pale and withdrawn, and they would whisper their own conclusions. That she was unhappy. That the formidable Duke of Ice was too much for her delicate constitution. The irony, a bitter, scalding thing, was that for once, they were not entirely wrong. She *was* unhappy. But I, her husband, was as ignorant of the true cause as they were.

Then came the aversion to food. At our silent, agonizing dinners, I began to notice she was not eating. She would allow the footmen to serve her, would lift her fork and knife and make a pretense of a meal, but she merely pushed the food around on her plate. A slice of rich venison, a spoonful of creamy sauce—it would all be left untouched. She subsisted on dry toast and weak tea, her appetite seemingly vanished.

The memory of my first night at Ravenswood, when my aunt had made a hopeful, jesting remark about the cause of her pallor, returned to me. The thought of a child, of an heir, flickered at the edge of my mind, a brief, treacherous spark of the hope I had allowed myself to feel in the country.

But I extinguished it immediately. It was impossible. Our nights, since that fevered encounter in the carriage, had resumed, but they were strange, disconnected affairs. She would come to my bed, a silent and dutiful ghost, and in a surprising, almost desperate shift, she had lately taken the lead, her body moving atop mine with a frantic energy that felt more like a flight from something than a surrender to me.

I had felt it then, in the darkness—the strange, unfamiliar firmness of her belly beneath my hands. It was a detail that puzzled me, but the notion of a child was a fleeting absurdity. Impossible. My experience with Violetta's pregnancy had been one of immediate and complete separation; she had retreated to her own chambers, citing a woman's delicacy, and our marital duties had ceased entirely. In my mind, pregnancy was a state of retreat and fragility. A woman in such a condition would surely not possess the strength or the desire for the vigorous, almost wild passion my wife had shown.

No, there had to be another explanation.

My mind, a cold and logical engine, seized on the only one that fit the facts as I knew them. Her grief. The "precious someone" she had lost, the living ghost her family had lied to her about. Her sorrow was not a simple, quiet mourning; it was a sickness, a physical malady that was consuming her from the inside out. It was draining her strength, stealing her appetite, turning her into this pale, fragile creature who was fading before my very eyes.

The thought of it, of her so consumed by a passion for another man that it was physically destroying her, ignited a fresh wave of a jealousy so fierce it was almost a physical pain. I was her husband. I was the man who had given her his name, his protection. And yet, I was powerless against this phantom rival, this secret she guarded more fiercely than a dragon guarding its treasure.

I could not let it continue. Her visible decline was becoming a liability, a weakness that my political enemies could, and would, exploit. But more than that, a part of me, the man who had held her as she wept in the chapel, could not bear to watch her suffer. I had to breach the wall. I had to try.

I chose my moment carefully. It was a rare, quiet evening. We had no social obligations. I found her in the library after dinner, staring out the tall window at the darkening city skyline. The book she had been holding had slipped to the floor, forgotten.

"Marietta," I said, my voice softer than I intended.

AN UNSPOKEN SUSPICION

She started, turning from the window, her hand flying to her throat in a now-familiar gesture of startled defense. "Your Grace," she murmured, her eyes wide and guarded.

I walked towards her, stopping a few feet away, keeping a careful, unthreatening distance. "You are unwell," I stated. It was not a question. It was an observation, a fact that had become undeniable. "You are not eating. You are tired. Forgive me for intruding on your privacy, but as your husband, I must insist on knowing the cause."

I saw a flicker of pure, unadulterated panic in her eyes. She looked like a cornered animal, desperately searching for an escape route. "It is nothing," she said, her voice a high, thin thing that was utterly unconvincing. "A lingering chill from our journey, perhaps. Or a headache. I am perfectly well."

Her lies were a wall of glass—transparent, yet impenetrable. I could see the truth she was hiding, the raw, profound sorrow in her eyes, but she would not allow me to touch it.

"A chill that lasts for weeks?" I pressed, my patience beginning to fray. "A headache that steals your appetite and leaves you as pale as a ghost? I am not a fool, Marietta. Something is deeply wrong. Is it... him? Is your grief for this man so great that it is making you ill?"

The moment the words left my mouth, I saw her recoil as if I had struck her. Her face, already pale, went ashen. I had guessed correctly. I had named her secret sorrow. And her reaction was not one of relief, of a burden finally shared. It was one of pure, shuttered terror.

"You couldn't possibly understand," she whispered, her voice trembling. She wrapped her arms around herself, a gesture of desperate self-protection. "Please. Leave me be."

Her dismissal, her absolute refusal to let me in, even when her own health was failing, was a final, damning confirmation. Her heart was a fortress dedicated to the memory of another man, and I was, and would always be, the enemy at the gates.

A cold, familiar fury rose in me, but I forced it down. Anger had gained me nothing but a night of desperate, meaningless passion. I would try a different

65

tactic.

"Very well," I said, my voice the cool, formal instrument of the Duke once more. I retreated, putting the physical distance between us that she so clearly craved. "If you will not confide in me, you will confide in a physician. I will not have my Duchess fading away before my eyes. I will send for Dr. Arbuthnot in the morning."

The panic in her eyes intensified. "No!" she cried, the word a sharp, desperate sound. "No doctors. I forbid it. I am fine. It is just... a woman's malady. It will pass."

Her vehemence, her absolute terror at the thought of a physician, was the final, baffling piece of the puzzle. What was she so afraid of a doctor discovering? Was her secret grief so profound that she feared a doctor might deem her mad, melancholic?

I did not know. I only knew that I was trapped in a marriage with a woman who was a stranger to me, a woman whose secrets were a sickness that was consuming her, a woman who would rather waste away than grant me even the smallest measure of her trust.

"As you wish," I said, my voice as cold as the grave. I turned and walked from the room, leaving her to her ghosts. But my suspicion, a cold and watchful thing, had taken on a new, sharper edge. She was not just hiding her grief from me. She was hiding something more. And I, her husband, the man whose name she bore, was now more determined than ever to discover what it was.

12

A Stolen Afternoon

Callum

The picnic was, like most of our public life, a necessary lie. The Duke and Duchess of Highmoor were patrons of a new public garden, and our attendance at its inaugural fete was a command performance. We sat upon a tartan blanket under the shade of a sprawling oak, a picture of domestic tranquility for the benefit of the reporters from the society pages and the watchful eyes of the *ton*. A wicker basket filled with an untouched luncheon sat beside us, the scent of roasted chicken and sweet strawberries a mockery of the bitter, unspoken truths between us.

Marietta was paler than usual, the dappled sunlight filtering through the leaves only serving to emphasize the bruised, purple shadows beneath her eyes. She had been pushing herself relentlessly, a whirlwind of ducal duties, and the strain was etched on every line of her delicate face. She smiled, she made polite, distant conversation, but I could see the effort it cost her. She was a fragile porcelain doll, and I could see the cracks beginning to form.

My own emotions were a maelstrom of frustration and a fierce, unwelcome protectiveness. I watched as she took a small, obligatory bite of a cucumber sandwich, saw the way her throat worked as she forced it down, the faint sheen of sweat on her brow. This was not the act of a woman enjoying a summer afternoon. This was an endurance test.

"You should rest," I said, my voice a low murmur, pitched only for her ears. She gave a small, startled shake of her head. "I am perfectly well."

"You are a terrible liar, Duchess," I countered, the title a soft rebuke. I gestured to the blanket. "Lie down. Rest your head. Anyone watching will simply assume you are fatigued from the sun. It is a perfectly acceptable wifely weakness."

I saw the conflict in her eyes. The need to maintain her perfect, strong façade warring with the genuine illness she was so determined to deny. With a small, weary sigh of surrender, she acquiesced. She lay down on the blanket, her movements stiff and careful, and after a moment's hesitation, she rested her head in my lap.

The moment she did, the world seemed to shift. The polite chatter of the party, the distant laughter of children, it all faded to a dull, meaningless hum. My world narrowed to the woman lying before me. Her head was a warm, living weight on my thighs. A few stray tendrils of her dark, silky hair had come loose from their pins and lay against the dark wool of my trousers, the contrast a thing of startling, painful beauty. I could smell the faint, clean scent of her, of lavender and woman, a scent that was seared into my memory from a single, chaotic night in an inn room.

My hand, as if with a will of its own, lifted. I meant only to brush a stray lock of hair from her cheek. But the moment my fingers touched her skin, a jolt, a current of pure, unadulterated sensation, shot through me. Her skin was as soft as a rose petal, and cool to the touch, belying the feverish intensity that I knew simmered just beneath the surface.

She did not pull away. Her eyes, which had been closed, fluttered open. She looked up at me, her green eyes wide and vulnerable, a silent question in their depths. And in that moment, in the dappled sunlight of a public park, the fragile truce we had been attempting was annihilated, not by anger, but by a desire so powerful, so immediate, it stole the air from my lungs.

I forgot the reporters. I forgot the gossips. I forgot the ghost of the man who stood between us. I forgot everything but the feel of her skin beneath my fingertips, the scent of her hair, the parted, questioning curve of her lips.

I lowered my head, slowly, giving her every opportunity to turn away, to reject me. But she did not. She simply watched me, her green eyes wide and vulnerable in the dappled sunlight, her breath catching in a small, audible gasp. And then my mouth was on hers.

The kiss was not like the bruising, angry kiss in the dining room. It was an act of profound, aching tenderness, a question and a confession all in one. Her head was still resting in my lap, forcing me to lean over her, a gesture that felt both protective and deeply reverent. I could not be demanding from this angle; I could only offer. I brushed my lips against hers, a soft, feather-light touch, at first.

It was a taste of the hope I had so foolishly allowed myself to feel that morning in the inn. Her lips were soft, hesitant, and they trembled slightly under mine. I deepened the kiss gently, tilting my head to better fit my mouth to hers. I felt her sigh, a soft sound of surrender that seemed to travel directly into my soul. She parted her lips for me, a silent, willing invitation that sent a fresh wave of fire through my veins. It was a sweet, languid exploration, a slow dance of tongues in the warm afternoon air, a promise whispered without a single word.

It was a long, slow, deep kiss, a conversation our words could no longer have. I poured all my frustration, all my confusion, all my desperate, undeniable longing for her into it. And she, in turn, seemed to pour all her secret sorrow, all her loneliness, into her response.

I felt her hand come up to cup my jaw, her thumb stroking my cheek, a gesture of such surprising, gentle intimacy that a low groan rumbled in my chest. This was not the act of a woman whose heart belonged to another. This was the act of a woman who was just as lost, just as hungry, as I was.

I broke the kiss, my breathing ragged. We stared at each other for a long, silent moment, the world rushing back in around us. Her face was flushed, her lips swollen, her eyes dark with the same raw desire that was coursing through my own veins.

Before another word could be spoken, she sat up, her movements quick and flustered. She looked around, her eyes wide with a dawning panic as she remembered where we were, in full view of half the *ton*. "We cannot," she whispered, her voice trembling.

But it was too late. The fire had been lit. My gaze swept the grounds, past the manicured lawns and polite clusters of guests, to a small, overgrown hill at the edge of the woods. Upon it stood a folly, a small Grecian temple of white stone, half-swallowed by ivy and forgotten by time. It was perfectly secluded.

"That folly," I said, my voice a low, commanding growl. "No one ever goes there." It was not a request. It was a statement of intent.

I stood and helped her to her feet, my hand lingering at her waist. I did not bother with excuses to our host; we simply gathered our blanket as if preparing to leave, and began to walk, not towards the line of waiting carriages, but away from the crowd, towards the hill. Each step was a silent, charged agreement, a shared conspiracy that made my heart hammer in my chest.

The air grew cooler as we entered the shade of the trees. The folly was even more dilapidated up close, the stone weathered and stained, wild roses climbing its columns in a riot of untamed beauty. The heavy wooden door groaned in protest as I pushed it open, revealing a small, circular room. Dust motes danced in the shafts of sunlight that pierced the grimy windows. In the center of the room, draped in a dusty canvas, was a stone bench. It was a secret, forgotten place, a perfect sanctuary for what was to come.

The moment the door closed behind us, sealing us away from the world, I was on her. I pressed her back against the cool, rough stone of the wall, my mouth finding hers again, this time with a desperate, claiming hunger. She met me with a fervor that stole the air from my lungs, her hands tangling in my hair, her body melting against mine.

I kissed her, my hands sliding from her waist to cup her face, my thumbs tracing the elegant line of her jaw. She was so exquisitely beautiful, so maddeningly complex, and in this moment, she was mine.

I broke the kiss only to trail a line of hot, open-mouthed kisses down her throat. I felt the frantic, bird-like flutter of her pulse beneath my lips, a testament to the passion she could not, or would not, name.

"You make me lose my mind," I growled against her skin.

70

"You are already mad," she whispered back, a breathless, broken sound, and then she was kissing me again, a wild, beautiful creature who had finally, for this one stolen afternoon, surrendered to the storm.

My hands were no longer content with her face, her throat. I needed more. I needed all of her. My fingers found the row of tiny buttons at the back of her afternoon dress, my movements clumsy with an urgency that bordered on desperation.

She did not stop me. She leaned into me, her own hands working at the buttons of my waistcoat, her touch a brand against my chest. This was not a rejection. This was a mutual, desperate, and undeniable need.

I finally freed her from the confines of her dress, letting it pool in a cloud of muslin at her feet. She stood before me in her chemise and corset, a pale, beautiful statue in the dappled sunlight. This time, there was no anger. There was only a desperate, aching tenderness. I undressed her slowly, worshipping every inch of her pale, perfect skin with my mouth and my hands.

As I unlaced her corset, freeing her breasts, I paused. They were fuller, heavier in my palms than I remembered, the areolas a darker, richer rose. The change was subtle, but undeniable, a new ripeness that sent a fresh jolt of possessive fire through me.

I did not move on. I lowered my head, my tongue tracing the edge of the darker aureole before my mouth closed over the peak. She gasped, a sharp, ragged sound, her back arching off the dusty canvas. The taste of her was clean and sweet, a taste of woman and of sunlight. I suckled, drawing the hardened nub deep into my mouth, and she let out a low, helpless moan that was the most beautiful sound I had ever heard. Her fingers, which had been resting on my shoulders, tangled convulsively in my hair, holding me to her. A fierce, possessive satisfaction surged through me. This new fullness was a welcome change, a ripeness I found deeply, powerfully arousing.

Sated for the moment, I moved to the other breast, giving it the same devoted attention until she was writhing beneath me, her breath coming in short, panting sobs of pleasure. Only then did I continue my exploration, my mouth trailing a path of fire down her ribs as I learned the shape of her, the taste of her, the sounds she made when my fingers found the wet, secret heat of her.

And she, in turn, explored me with a shy, wondering curiosity, her hands tracing the muscles of my chest, her lips following the path of her fingers. She was not a passive recipient of my passion; she was an active, willing participant, a woman claiming her own pleasure, her own desire.

After I had worshipped her breasts until she was a writhing, whimpering creature against me, my hands moved lower, sliding down the soft skin of her belly. She gasped as my fingers tangled in the dark curls at the juncture of her thighs, her hips instinctively pressing against my hand. She was so exquisitely ready for me, her desire a hot, wet welcome to my touch. I explored her with a slow, devastating confidence, my fingers stroking, circling, until she was panting, her head thrown back, a single, perfect tear of pure sensation tracing a path by her temple.

That was all I needed. Without breaking our kiss, I braced myself, my hands moving to grip her waist. I lifted her, and her body, impossibly light, moved with a perfect, trusting instinct, her legs wrapping around my waist, her ankles locking behind my back.

I entered her then, pressing her back against the solid wall, my body supporting hers. It was a single, deep, and perfect thrust that joined us completely. She gasped into my mouth, her body closing around me, a hot, wet glove of pure sensation. The feel of her, clinging to me, taking all of me, was an assault on the senses, a beautiful, perfect madness.

I began to move, my thrusts powerful and steady, our bodies finding a rhythm that was raw and primal. It was a rough, fast, and desperate coupling, a physical expression of all the anger and the longing that we could not put into words. Every thrust was a claim, every arch of her hips against the wall a surrender. She clung to me, her legs wrapped tightly around me, her whispered cries mingling with my own ragged breaths. The world outside, with its sun and its gardens and its secrets, ceased to exist. There was only this. This stolen, frantic, and beautiful oblivion.

The pleasure built, a relentless, rising tide, and I felt her body begin to convulse around me, her inner muscles clenching in a wave of pure, shattering ecstasy. I followed her over the edge, my own release a violent, shuddering wave, my name a torn, ragged cry on her lips.

In the aftermath, I held her, my muscles trembling with the effort, her body a warm, pliant weight in my arms. Her head rested in the hollow of my shoulder, her breathing slowly returning to a steady rhythm. The silence that fell was not a hostile thing. It was a peaceful, sated quiet, broken only by the sound of a distant bird singing outside the folly walls.

Carefully, I carried her the few steps to the dusty stone bench and gently laid her down, pulling the rough canvas over her for warmth before lying beside her on the narrow space, gathering her into my arms.

My hand, which had been stroking her hair, drifted lower, down the elegant line of her spine, over the soft curve of her hip. My fingers moved to her stomach, intending to trace idle patterns on the soft skin there. As my palm flattened against her, I registered something unexpected—not a curve, but a subtle, unfamiliar firmness low in her abdomen, a tautness beneath the soft skin that had not been there before.

She flinched.

It was not a large movement. It was a sudden, violent tightening of her muscles, a sharp, indrawn breath that was not of pleasure. Her entire body went rigid in my arms.

I froze, my hand hovering over her skin, the strange firmness I'd just felt forgotten, eclipsed by the raw terror in her reaction. The fire in my veins turned to ice. "Marietta?"

She squeezed her eyes shut, a look of pure, unadulterated terror on her face. She looked at me as if I were a monster.

I withdrew my hand as if I had been burned. The sudden, violent tension in her body was a stark rejection, made all the more brutal coming immediately after such profound intimacy. The fire in my veins turned to ice.

My mind struggled to reconcile the contradiction. She had come to me willingly. She had met my passion with a fire that was fierce and genuine, undeniable. And yet, the moment my hand rested on her stomach—a simple, possessive gesture, a husband's quiet claim in the aftermath—she had recoiled as if struck.

I saw it then, a different, colder truth. The passion had been real, yes, a physical storm we both craved. But my touch afterward, that simple claim of ownership... that was what she could not bear. Because ownership implies a future, a belonging. And her future, the deepest loyalty of her being, was still sworn to another. The ghost of Thorne.

Her flinch was not about illness. It was about allegiance. That explained the fatigue, the nausea, the constant, weary sorrow—the physical toll of a woman living a lie, her body bound to one man while her heart remained fiercely loyal to another. She wasn't hiding an illness; she was resisting the cage.

I held her a little tighter, a fierce, protective ache mixing with the bitter taste of my own inadequacy. I did not have her heart. Not yet. Perhaps never. But I had her body, willing or not in these quiet moments. And for now, in this fragile, stolen peace, it would have to be enough.

13

A Moment of Hope

Marietta

I n the quiet, dusty aftermath, with the sun slanting through the grimy windows of the forgotten folly, a fragile peace settled over me. I lay in his arms on the narrow stone bench, the rough canvas a strange counterpoint to the impossible softness I felt in my heart. The storm of our passion had passed, and in its wake, it had left not the cold, desolate silence I had come to expect, but a quiet, trembling tenderness.

He shifted, his body a warm, solid weight against mine. "We should go," he murmured, his voice a low, rough thing against my hair. "Before they send out a search party for their lost Duchess."

A small laugh escaped my lips. "They would search for their Duke first."

He smiled, a slow, genuine smile that I felt more than saw. He helped me to my feet, his hands gentle on my arms, his gaze soft and unguarded. The world felt new, as if I were seeing it, and him, for the very first time.

My clothes were a soft pile of muslin on the floor. As I reached for my chemise, he stopped me, his hand closing gently over mine.

"Allow me," he said, his voice a quiet rumble.

My heart gave a soft, fluttering leap. I stood before him as he retrieved my corset, a garment that had always felt like a cage, a symbol of my restriction.

But when he held it, it seemed like something else entirely. He turned me so my back was to him, and I felt the cool press of the boning against my skin. His fingers, so large and strong, were surprisingly deft as he began to thread the laces.

His touch was a ghost of a caress against my bare skin, sending shivers of a new, quieter pleasure through me. The air was thick with a new kind of intimacy, more profound than the fire of our passion. His warm breath ghosted across my shoulder as he worked.

"Callum," I whispered, my voice a little breathless. "I believe we have had quite enough intimacy for one afternoon."

I felt his lips press against the sensitive skin of my nape, a soft, warm kiss that made my knees feel weak. "I am not making love to you, Marietta," he murmured against my shoulder, his voice a low, thrilling vibration. "I am simply kissing my wife."

He continued his sweet, leisurely assault as he tightened the laces, his mouth trailing a path of fire over my shoulder blade, his lips finding the curve of my neck. Each touch was a silent promise, a gentle apology, a declaration of a new beginning. When he was finished, he turned me in his arms, his grey eyes dark with an emotion so tender it made my heart ache.

He helped me with my dress, his hands lingering at my waist, and then, taking my hand in his, he led me from the dusty sanctuary of the folly and back out into the bright, unforgiving light of the world. His hand in mine felt impossibly right, a warm, solid anchor in the swirling confusion of my own heart. For the first time, I allowed myself a dangerous indulgence: I allowed myself to hope.

As we emerged from the shade of the trees onto the main lawn, a familiar voice called out to us. It was the old Baron Ashworth and his wife, a kindly, elderly couple who had known Callum's family for generations.

"There you are, Your Grace!" the Baron boomed, his face wreathed in a good-natured smile. "Her Ladyship and I were just remarking that you and your lovely Duchess had vanished. Stealing a moment away from the crowd, eh?"

I felt a flush creep up my neck, but Callum's hand gave mine a reassuring squeeze. Lady Ashworth tapped her husband's arm with her fan, though her own eyes were sparkling with amusement. "Hush, Arthur. Do not tease them. One must make time for such things when one is newly married." Her gaze, warm and maternal, shifted to me. "It does my heart good to see you both looking so well. We shall expect to hear happy news before the year is out, I am certain."

The casual, well-meaning words were a jolt, a sudden, cold reminder of the secret I carried. I tensed, but Callum seemed not to notice my sudden chill. Instead, a genuine, warm smile spread across his face, a smile so full of uncomplicated joy it was the most beautiful thing I had ever seen.

"We are both most eager for that day, my lady," he said, his voice holding a warmth that seemed to envelop me. "I find I cannot wait to be a father."

His words, spoken so openly and with such genuine, uncomplicated joy, sent a jolt through my heart. It was a beautiful, aching hope and a cold wave of panic, all at once. He was speaking of a future I was already secretly living, a dream he did not know had already begun. A blush rose to my cheeks, and I lowered my gaze, a perfect imitation of a shy, happy bride. My free hand, as if with a will of its own, came to rest on my lower abdomen, a quiet, unconscious gesture of protection and of connection to the tiny life I carried within.

The couple beamed, their teasing validated by what they surely saw as my hopeful, maternal gesture. After a few more pleasantries and knowing smiles, they moved on, leaving us alone on the path.

The moment was perfect, the air was warm, and the man beside me, my husband, was looking at me with an expression of such open, tender affection that it made my heart ache with a love so fierce it was almost painful.

He pulled me closer, his arm circling my waist, turning me to face him. The memory of our passion, of the new, subtle ripeness of my body, was a fresh, potent fire in his eyes. He lowered his head, his lips finding the shell of my ear. His free hand came to rest on my abdomen, on the soft, still-flat plain of my stomach, a gesture of pure, hopeful possession.

"Heed her words, my love," he whispered, his voice a soft, intimate thing meant only for her. "I am waiting, most impatiently, for you to conceive our child."

The world stopped.

His words, meant as the most profound declaration of love and hope, were a sentence of doom. His touch, so full of a husband's tender longing, was a brand of pure terror on my skin. A wave of guilt, so profound it was sickening, crashed over me. He spoke with such innocent eagerness about his dream of becoming a father, and all the while, I was the one keeping him from the truth. He was waiting for a child I already carried. The deception, the sheer scale of the wrong I was doing to this good, honorable man in this moment of his perfect hope, was a sin I was not sure I could ever be forgiven for.

Every fear I had ever harbored, every ghost of my past, rose up in a single, silent scream. The fragile, beautiful moment shattered into a million pieces. I could not breathe. I could not move. I went rigid in his arms, my body instantly transformed from a pliant, warm creature into a statue of pure, frozen terror.

He pulled back, and I felt his entire body tense with a dawning, terrible confusion. I looked up at him, my face a mask I could no longer control. The soft, happy flush was gone. In its place was a deathly pallor. My eyes, which had just been shining with a gentle warmth, were now wide with a look of pure, unadulterated panic. His hopeful, loving words had not been a comfort. They had been a threat.

The beautiful, perfect moment was shattered. I was once again a stranger, a woman of secrets and shadows, and I was left utterly, devastatingly, and completely in the dark.

14

An Unexpected Arrival

Marietta

The stolen afternoon in the park was a beautiful, fleeting mirage in the vast, arid desert of our marriage. For a few, precious hours, the walls between us had crumbled, and we had found a desperate, passionate solace in each other's arms. I had gone to him willingly, my body betraying my cautious mind, and in the heat of his embrace, I had allowed myself to hope. I had seen not a suspicious adversary, but a man of deep, aching want, a man as lonely as I was. In the sated, peaceful silence that followed, I had dared to believe that this, perhaps, was a new beginning.

The illusion, like all beautiful things in my life, did not last. The moment we returned to the cold, formal grandeur of Redwyck House, the masks were once again in place. The passion we had shared became an unspoken, unacknowledged ghost that haunted the silent corridors between our separate chambers. He did not come to my room that night, nor the night after. The fragile, physical bridge we had built had led nowhere.

He was not as cold as before, but a new, more complex barrier had been erected. His watchfulness intensified. He would look at me across the dinner table with a strange, unreadable expression, a mixture of the desire I knew he felt and a deep, confounding sorrow. He was a man wrestling with a ghost, and I, in my ignorance, had come to believe that the ghost was his first wife, the tragic Violetta, her memory a constant, silent chaperone to our every interaction. I believed he felt guilty for the passion he felt for me, that his heart was a battlefield between the dead woman he had once loved and the living one he was reluctantly bound to.

The irony, a cruel and constant companion, was that he was indeed wrestling with a ghost—but it was mine, not his. A ghost he had invented, a phantom lover for whom he believed I still grieved. And I, in my cowardice, in my desperate need to protect my daughter, could do nothing to exorcise it.

Our days settled back into the familiar, fragile façade. We were the perfect Duke and Duchess, our public performances flawless, our private life a wasteland of silent, aching misunderstanding. And all the while, the secret I carried grew within me, a silent, steady heartbeat that was both a profound joy and a constant, terrifying accusation.

The summons arrived on a Tuesday, a day like any other, a day of quiet, ducal routine. I was in the morning room, reviewing the household accounts with Mrs. Finch, the endless columns of numbers a welcome, logical distraction from the chaotic, illogical state of my heart.

A footman entered, his face impassive as he presented a sealed note on a silver salver. "An urgent message for His Grace, Your Grace," he said. "And the messenger indicated it is for your eyes as well."

I took the note, my brow furrowing in mild curiosity. It was not from a government office. The wax seal was a simple, elegant 'T'. I broke it, my eyes scanning the beautiful, familiar, flowing script.

My Dearest Callum & Marietta,

Forgive the short notice, but I find I simply cannot bear the silence of the country any longer! The season is in full swing, and a foolish old woman has decided she craves a bit of city excitement. Expect Isabelle and me to descend upon you tomorrow afternoon. Do not trouble yourself with any grand preparations—we shall be perfectly content to be tucked away in a quiet corner of your grand mausoleum. I am so looking forward to seeing you both, and my little darling has spoken of nothing but her 'Aunt Marietta' for weeks!

With deepest affection,

Your Aunt Tamsin

The note fluttered from my numb fingers, landing with a soft, whispery sound on the polished mahogany of the table. The columns of numbers in the account book swam before my eyes, dissolving into a meaningless blur. The air in the room, once so calm and orderly, was suddenly thin, unbreathable.

They were coming. Here.

My mind, a slow, terrified engine, struggled to process the information. Lady Tamsin and Isabelle. Not at Ravenswood, a safe, distant haven of golden memories. They were coming to London. To Redwyck House. To this cold, silent fortress of secrets and suspicion. My daughter was going to be living under the same roof as my husband.

A wave of pure, unadulterated terror, so powerful it was like a physical blow, crashed over me. It was followed immediately by a surge of joy so fierce, so possessive, it was almost a form of madness. My daughter. I was going to see my daughter again. I would be able to touch her, to read to her, to hear her laughter echoing in these silent, lonely halls. The thought was a glimpse of heaven.

But this house was not heaven. It was a gilded cage, ruled by a man who was my silent, watchful adversary. A man who was already consumed by a suspicion I could not name. To bring Isabelle here, into this charged, poisoned atmosphere, was to bring a fragile, beautiful wildflower into the heart of a glacier.

Mrs. Finch's voice cut through the roaring in my ears. "Is everything alright, Your Grace? You have gone quite pale."

I looked at her, my eyes wide and unseeing. I had to compose myself. I had to be the Duchess. "It is... unexpected news, Mrs. Finch," I managed to say, my voice a high, thin sound I barely recognized. "His Grace's aunt, Lady Tamsin, and her ward are arriving for an extended visit. Tomorrow."

The housekeeper's expertly trained composure did not falter, but I saw a flicker of surprise in her eyes. "Very good, Your Grace. I shall have the west wing guest chambers prepared at once."

She began to turn, but I stopped her. "And Mrs. Finch," I added, my voice gaining a strange, new urgency. "Please, speak with the cook. I want a special tea prepared for their arrival. See that he bakes a selection of cakes and biscuits for... for the child."

The housekeeper paused, turning back to me. "Of course, Your Grace. Does the young lady have any particular favorites you are aware of?"

The simple, logical question sent a fresh pang of sorrow through me. I did not know my own daughter's favorite cake. The thought was a small, sharp agony. A flicker of sadness must have crossed my face, for I saw a look of gentle confusion in Mrs. Finch's eyes before I masked it. I looked away, as if searching my memory.

"I am not certain," I said, the lie tasting like ash. Then, an image, a feeling, a pure maternal instinct rose unbidden within me. "But... have him prepare a sponge cake with fresh strawberries. And small lemon biscuits, shaped like stars if he is able. I have a feeling she would like that. It is most important that she feels very welcome here."

Mrs. Finch's expression softened. "That sounds delightful, Your Grace. I will see to it personally."

"Thank you, Mrs. Finch," I said, my voice trembling slightly. "That will be all."

She gave a crisp curtsy and retreated, leaving me alone with the letter and the catastrophic, beautiful news it contained. I sank back into my chair, my face in my hands, my body shaking with a storm of conflicting emotions. Joy. Terror. A wild, irrational hope. A profound, soul-deep dread.

This was a blessing. This was a curse. This was a test I was not sure I had the strength to endure.

They arrived the following afternoon, a whirlwind of trunks and chatter and life that seemed to momentarily banish the oppressive gloom of Redwyck House. Lady Tamsin was a force of nature, her warm, affectionate energy a stark contrast to the cold formality of our home. She embraced me as if I were her own daughter, her bright, intelligent eyes crinkling at the corners as she declared that the city air had not been kind to me and that I was far too thin. And then, there was Isabelle.

She stood just inside the grand hall, a small, perfect figure in a navy blue traveling cloak, her dark curls peeking out from under the brim of her bonnet. She clutched a worn, beloved doll in one hand, her wide green eyes, *my* green eyes, taking in the vast, intimidating space with a solemn, shy curiosity.

Our eyes met across the cavernous hall, and in that moment, the world fell away. There was only my child. My daughter. My heart gave a painful, lurching thud against my ribs, a desperate, maternal cry that I was forced to hold in silence.

"Aunt Marietta!" she cried, her shyness overcome by a sudden, joyful recognition. She dropped her doll and ran, her small feet pattering on the cold marble floor, and launched herself into my arms.

I knelt, catching her, my own arms wrapping around her in a fierce, desperate embrace. I buried my face in her hair, inhaling the sweet, familiar scent of her, the scent I had dreamed of for weeks. The feel of her small, warm body in my arms was a physical shock, a jolt of pure, agonizing joy that was so intense it was almost unbearable. For a few, precious, stolen seconds, I was not the Duchess. I was not a wife. I was a mother, holding her child.

It was the sound of Callum clearing his throat that broke the spell.

I looked up, my vision blurred by a sudden, hot rush of tears I had to blink back. He was standing by the fireplace, where he had been waiting to greet his aunt. He had not moved. He was a tall, formidable statue of a man, his face a mask of cool, unreadable civility. But his eyes... his eyes were fixed on us, on me and the child in my arms, and they were not the eyes of a fond uncle.

They were the eyes of a prosecutor watching a defendant, cold, analytical, and deeply, profoundly suspicious.

I realized then, with a fresh wave of cold terror, how this must look to him. He saw his wife, a woman he believed was grieving for a secret lover, clinging to a child with a desperate, tearful intensity that went far beyond the bounds of a normal aunt's affection. He saw my joy, my raw, unguarded emotion, and he did not see it as a blessing.

He saw it as proof.

Proof of the deep, secret, and passionate nature he believed I was hiding from him. He saw Isabelle, not as his aunt's charming ward, but as a living, breathing symbol of the past I would not relinquish, of the ghost he could not defeat. He saw her as the living embodiment of my betrayal.

The joy that had filled my heart curdled into a cold, sickening dread. I gently unwrapped Isabelle's arms from around my neck, my own hands trembling. I stood, pulling the mask of the serene Duchess back into place, a polite, meaningless smile on my lips.

"Welcome to Redwyck House, Isabelle," I said, my voice a stranger's, a formal, distant thing.

I turned to my husband, the smile feeling brittle and false on my face. "Isn't this a wonderful surprise, Your Grace?"

He did not smile back. He simply watched us, his gaze a heavy, judging weight. "Indeed," he said, his voice as cold and as unforgiving as the marble beneath my feet. "A surprise."

The battle had come home. The source of my greatest joy and my deepest secret was now here, in this house, under the constant, watchful, and deeply suspicious gaze of my husband. I was no longer just walking on a knife's edge. I was trapped in a room with a sleeping lion, and I had just brought him the one thing that was certain to wake him.

15

The Fainting

Callum

For two days, I observed my wife's metamorphosis, and I found myself utterly confounded. The pale, silent Duchess who haunted the halls of Redwyck House had vanished upon our arrival in London. In her place was a woman I did not recognize, a creature of light and baffling energy, and the catalyst for this transformation was the child, Isabelle.

I was fond of the girl myself. It was impossible not to be. She was a charming and clever child, with a shy smile and my wife's impossible green eyes—a fact I noted with a distant, familial pride. She was my cousin now, a Redwyck in all but blood, and I found a quiet pleasure in her presence. She brought a warmth to the cold, formal corridors of my home that had been absent for a very long time.

But Marietta's reaction to her was something else entirely. It was... unsettling. My wife, who so often moved through our life with the quiet, weary grace of a sleepwalker, was suddenly, startlingly awake. She, who barely spoke a word to me over dinner, would chatter endlessly with the child, her voice a soft, melodic sound I had not heard since our brief truce at Ravenswood. On the first morning, she had personally instructed the cook to prepare lemon biscuits shaped like stars, claiming with a strange certainty that she was sure the child would enjoy them, and had been proven right when Isabelle devoured them with delighted giggles.

I would watch from the doorway of the morning room as Marietta knelt to spoon jam onto Isabelle's toast, her face alight with a smile of such profound, tender focus it was unnerving. She would play with her for hours in the nursery, their shared laughter a constant, beautiful, and strangely isolating sound. I felt a pang of something I could only identify as a ridiculous, foolish jealousy. It was absurd to be jealous of a child, and yet, I could not deny the strange, uneasy feeling that settled in my gut as I watched them. They created a world of their own, a perfect, sunlit bubble into which I could not enter. They had a bond that was immediate, absolute, and utterly baffling.

The breaking point came on the third day of their visit. It was a bright, cool afternoon, and I was in my study, attempting to focus on a stack of dispatches from Westminster. But my attention was fractured, my gaze drawn again and again to the tall window that overlooked the west lawn.

They were out there, playing a game of tag. Isabelle, a small whirlwind in a pale blue dress, shrieked with delighted laughter as she ran, her dark curls bouncing. And Marietta... my wife, who I had only ever seen walk with a slow, measured dignity, was running across the lawn, her own face flushed with exertion and a joy so pure and so unrestrained it was a thing of breathtaking beauty.

I watched, a silent, unseen observer, my heart a tight, aching knot in my chest. This was the woman from the inn. This was the woman from the folly. A woman of fire and of passion, a woman who had, for a few, precious, stolen moments, turned that light on me. And now, it was all for this child.

Isabelle stumbled and fell, as children do, and Marietta was there in an instant, scooping her up into her arms, swinging her around until the child's tears turned back into peals of laughter. She held the girl close, her face buried in her hair, and the look on her face was one of such fierce, agonizing love it stopped the very breath in my chest.

And then, I saw it.

The laughter died on her lips. The radiant color drained from her face, leaving her as pale as a death mask. She swayed on her feet, her grip on the child suddenly slack. She took one stumbling step, then another, her eyes wide and unfocused. And then, her knees buckled, and she collapsed onto the grass in a heap of pale green muslin.

I was moving before I had consciously registered the act. My chair crashed backward. I threw the study doors open and ran. The sight of Jennings, my butler, in the hall barely registering.

"Get Dr. Arbuthnot!" I bellowed, my voice a raw, unfamiliar sound of pure panic. "Now!"

I did not wait for his reply. I ran, shouting her name as I vaulted the low stone balustrade of the terrace. "Marietta!" I sprinted across the lawn, my own heart a cold, hard knot of terror in my chest, each beat a frantic prayer. *Not again. Please, not again.*

By the time I reached her, she was unconscious. Isabelle was kneeling beside her, her small body shaking with terrified sobs, pulling at her arm. "Aunt Marietta, wake up!"

A surge of pure, irrational anger shot through me, directed at the weeping child. *This was her fault. She had done this. She had pushed my wife to this state of exhaustion.*

"Go inside, Isabelle," I commanded, my voice a harsh, raw thing I barely recognized. "Find your Mama Tamsin. Now."

The child flinched at the sound of my voice and scrambled away, her sobs trailing behind her. I did not care. All that mattered was the still, silent woman at my feet. I gathered her limp, unconscious form into my arms, her body a fragile, weightless thing, and carried her back into the house, my own fear a silent, screaming chaos in my mind.

Dr. Arbuthnot arrived within the hour. After what felt like an eternity, he stepped out from her bedchamber, his expression serious, but the grim lines around his mouth had softened.

"The Duchess has regained consciousness," he said. "She is weak, but the immediate danger has passed."

A wave of relief so profound it almost buckled my knees washed over me. "What is it, man?" I demanded. "What is wrong with her?"

Dr. Arbuthnot's gaze met mine. "There is nothing 'wrong' with her, Your

Grace," he said quietly. "On the contrary." He paused, allowing the weight of his next words to settle. "Your Grace, the Duchess is with child. I would estimate she is nearly three months along."

The world stopped. *With child.* Three months. A surge of pure, unadulterated, triumphant joy so powerful it was like a physical blow, struck me. A child. An heir. My heir. Our passionate encounters had not been fruitless. They had been a beginning. I was to be a father.

But the doctor was still speaking, his voice a stern, warning note that cut through the haze of my elation. "However," he continued, "her collapse was a serious matter. She is suffering from profound exhaustion and, I would venture, a significant degree of emotional stress. It is a dangerous combination. Any further shocks or emotional upsets could be gravely dangerous. For both her, and for the child. She requires absolute rest and an absence of any agitation."

He looked from my face to my aunt's, his meaning clear. "She requires absolute rest. And a complete absence of any... agitation. Do I make myself clear?"

"Perfectly," I said, my voice a low, flat thing.

He gave a curt nod and left. I was left standing in the hallway, the doctor's words replaying in my mind. *Emotional stress... gravely dangerous... for the child.*

In that moment, the beautiful, incandescent joy of my impending fatherhood was instantly, horribly corrupted. I saw it all with a terrible, tragic certainty. I saw her in the garden, her face alight with that profound, unnatural, and obsessive affection for my aunt's ward. I saw her running, chasing, laughing until she collapsed.

The two events were inextricably linked. Her fainting, the event that was a direct physical threat to the future of my heir, had been triggered by the very "emotional stress" the doctor warned of—a stress born from her bizarre and intense attachment to Isabelle.

A strange, uneasy feeling, a feeling I could not name, settled in my gut. I was happy, of course. I was going to be a father. But my joy was overshadowed by this new, cold reality. The health of my wife, and the survival of my heir, was now tied to her baffling, obsessive connection to another child. And that, for reasons I could not yet comprehend, felt like a very dangerous thing indeed.

My joy curdled into a cold, protective fury. Her strange, secret obsession, whatever its root, was not just a source of my own confusion and jealousy. It was now a direct, physical threat to the life of my unborn child.

The choice was no longer about my own wounded pride. It was about my heir. The Redwyck heir. I would not allow her strange sorrows, her dangerous attachments, to threaten the future of my house.

I stared at the closed door of the room where my wife lay, and a new, cold resolve settled in my soul. I would protect my child. I would protect my legacy. And if that meant protecting them from the woman who carried them, and from the strange obsessions she refused to relinquish, then so be it. The war was no longer silent. It had just found its battlefield. And I would not lose.

16

A Father's Fear

Marietta

I drifted back to consciousness slowly, as if surfacing from a deep, dark body of water. The first thing I was aware of was the silence. Not the heavy, hostile silence of the dining room, but a soft, muffled quiet, the kind found in a sickroom. The second was the scent of lavender and clean, sun-dried linen.

I opened my eyes. I was not in the garden. I was in my own bed, in my chambers at Redwyck House, the heavy damask curtains drawn against the afternoon light, casting the room in a dim, peaceful twilight. A cool, damp cloth rested on my forehead. My body felt heavy, boneless, as if I had been asleep for a very long time.

The memory of what had happened came rushing back in a chaotic, terrifying flood. The west lawn, gleaming under the afternoon sun. The sound of Isabelle's shrieking laughter as we played tag. Scooping her up from the grass, the feel of her small, warm body in my arms as I swung her around. And then... the world tilting, the light fading, the sensation of falling into a bottomless blackness.

A small, panicked sound escaped my lips, and I tried to sit up, my mind instantly filled with a frantic, maternal terror. *Isabelle. Was she frightened?*

Was she hurt?

"Lie still." The voice, a low, quiet command, came from the shadows by the hearth.

Callum. He was sitting in the armchair, a book open but unread in his lap. He had been watching me. As my eyes adjusted to the dim light, I saw that the formidable Duke, the cold adversary, was gone. In his place was a man whose face was etched with a deep, profound exhaustion, and something else, something I could not name. A strange, guarded, and almost fearful intensity.

"The child is fine," he said, his voice flat, as if he had read my thoughts. "My aunt has her. She was not harmed." He paused. "You, however, collapsed."

"I... I am sorry," I whispered, my voice a hoarse, weak thing. "I do not know what came over me."

"I do," he said, and he rose from his chair and walked to my bedside. He stood over me, a tall, imposing figure, his shadow falling across the bed. "Dr. Arbuthnot has been here. He has explained the cause of your... illness."

My blood ran cold. The doctor. He had told him. The secret was out. I stared up at my husband, my heart a frantic, terrified drum against my ribs, bracing myself for the explosion, for the cold fury, for the accusations.

But the explosion never came. He simply looked at me, his grey eyes unreadable, his expression a mask of cool neutrality. And in that moment, I realized I did not know this man at all. I had no idea what he was thinking, what he was feeling.

"You are with child," he stated. It was not a question. It was a fact, a verdict delivered in a voice devoid of all emotion. He paused, and a flicker of something—not suspicion, but a strange, clinical thoughtfulness—crossed his features. "Perhaps you were unaware. The doctor says it is still quite early."

His words, meant perhaps as a strange sort of comfort, only highlighted the chasm between us. I could only nod, a single, mute admission, my gaze searching his for some flicker of the man who had held me at the inn, of the man who had smiled at me in the morning light. I found nothing.

"The doctor," he continued, his voice still that same, flat monotone, "was most explicit. Your condition is... delicate. You are suffering from exhaustion and emotional stress. Any further agitation could be gravely dangerous. For the child."

He said the last two words with a new, strange emphasis, and for the first time, I saw a flicker of emotion in his eyes. It was not the warmth I had so desperately hoped for. It was a fierce, cold, and almost obsessive protectiveness. A father's fear. But it was not directed at me. It was directed *through* me, at the unborn heir I carried.

In that moment, I ceased to be his wife. I ceased to be Marietta. I became a vessel. A fragile, necessary container for the future of the House of Redwyck.

His reaction was not one of rage or of tenderness. It was one of pure, ducal efficiency. The formidable, controlling Duke of Highmoor had been given a new, profoundly important project, and he would manage it with the same ruthless, single-minded focus with which he managed his political career and his vast estates.

That same afternoon, he turned from my bedside, his face a mask of cold resolve. He walked to the door of my chambers where a pale-faced Mrs. Finch was hovering, awaiting instructions.

"Mrs. Finch," he began, his voice quiet but unyielding, leaving no room for question. "The Duchess is to remain in her bed. She is not to be disturbed for any reason short of the house being on fire. Is that understood?"

"Yes, Your Grace," the housekeeper murmured, her eyes wide.

"Her meals will be only what Dr. Arbuthnot has prescribed. Nothing more. All correspondence that arrives for her is to be brought directly to me, unopened. All visitors, without exception, are to be turned away at the door. Her Grace is not at home to anyone."

"Very good, Your Grace," Mrs. Finch replied, though I saw a flicker of something—pity, perhaps—in her eyes as she glanced at me.

"The world outside this door is to be sealed," he concluded, his voice as cold and final as a tomb. "Her health, and the health of the heir, are now your primary and sole responsibility. You will not fail in it."

I heard his words from my bed, and a profound chill settled over me. *Her health, and the health of the heir.* He spoke of me as if I were a fragile piece of property to be guarded. But as the door closed, leaving me in the enforced quiet of my new prison, a strange and unexpected feeling bloomed in the center of my fear: relief. A single, heavy secret had been lifted.

My hand moved to my stomach. But now, in the privacy of my confinement, the gesture was different. It was no longer a furtive, fearful touch. For the first time in weeks, I could openly, lovingly, rub the gentle curve where our son rested.

"Oh, my sweetheart" I whispered to the silence, my voice thick with tears that were no longer of fear, but of a strange, fierce relief. "He knows. Your father knows you are here now. It is time for you to be loved." I pressed my palm more firmly against the swell, as if I could send my words directly to him. "Forgive me for hiding you. Forgive me for being so afraid."

I took a shuddering breath. I was a captive, yes, but I was no longer a liar about this one, most precious truth. My hand continued its slow, steady circles, a silent promise that I would keep him safe, not just from the agitations of the world, but from the cold, obsessive control of his own father.

And so, my convalescence began immediately, before the sun had even set on the day I had collapsed. I was placed under a strict, unyielding regimen of bed rest. My world shrank to the four walls of my bedchamber. My first meal of this new reality was brought to me on a tray—a simple, nourishing broth that had been personally approved by Dr. Arbuthnot. I was permitted to read, but only for an hour at a time, and only novels of a light, unchallenging nature. No newspapers. No letters. No contact with the outside world that might bring a single, agitating thought into my head.

At first, on that long and terrible day, I accepted it. I was weak, exhausted, and the quiet, muffled world of the sickroom was a strange sort of comfort. Callum himself oversaw every detail of my care with an obsessive, unnerving precision that began the moment the doctor left the house. He appeared in my room at scheduled intervals, his presence a silent, looming thing. He checked the temperature of my broth. He questioned the maids about the freshness of my linen. He stood by my bed, his gaze not on my face, but on my abdomen, as if he could will the child within me to be safe through the sheer force of his formidable will.

He was a perfect, attentive, and utterly impersonal nurse. He never touched me. He never spoke a word of affection, of tenderness. His concern was a clinical, cold thing, the concern of a master breeder for a prized and fragile mare. And as that first day bled into the next, and then into a week, his constant, watchful presence, his suffocating, obsessive care, began to feel less like a comfort and more like a cage.

The true cruelty, however, began on the second day. I awoke feeling a little stronger, and my first thought, my first desperate, aching need, was for Isabelle.

"I should like to see Isabelle," I said to him when he came for his morning inspection. "Perhaps she could come and sit with me for a little while. She could bring her book of fairy tales."

He froze, his hand hovering over the bellpull he had been about to ring. A strange, shuttered look came over his face. "That will not be possible," he said, his voice flat.

"But why?" I asked, a confused frown creasing my brow. "She would be quiet. She would not tire me. Her presence... it would be a comfort."

"The doctor was clear," he said, his voice taking on a hard, unyielding edge. "No agitation. The child is a... lively girl. Her energy would be a drain on your resources."

The excuse was so flimsy, so utterly nonsensical, that I could only stare at him in stunned disbelief. "She is a three-year-old girl, Callum, not a rampaging Cossack. She would be a comfort, not a trial."

"I have made my decision, Marietta," he said, and his voice was the voice of the Duke, a sound that brooked no argument. "You need to rest. Your focus must be entirely on your recovery. On the heir."

He turned and left the room, leaving me staring at the closed door, my mind reeling. It was not just a precaution. It was a decree. A banishment. He was forbidding my daughter from my sickroom.

To me, his actions seemed inexplicably, monstrously cruel. But when a distraught Lady Tamsin came to visit me later, I saw not just confusion in her eyes, but a deep, knowing sadness. My aunt-in-law was beside herself, her kind face a mask of sympathy and hurt.

"Oh, my dear child," she whispered, taking my hand in hers as she sat by my bed. "Isabelle is heartbroken, of course. She asks for her Aunt Marietta a dozen times a day and does not understand why she cannot see you."

Her words were a sharp, clean pain, cutting through the dull fog of my convalescence. My daughter was asking for me. The thought was a fresh, twisting agony in my chest. I gave a small, involuntary shake of my head, a silent protest against the cruelty of it, my gaze drifting to the window as if I could see my daughter's sad face reflected in the glass. I was lost in another universe of grief, and Lady Tamsin's voice seemed to come from a great distance.

She sighed, a sound of profound, weary understanding. "And he, that foolish, stubborn nephew of mine, has locked himself away in his study, convinced he is doing the right and honorable thing."

She looked at me, her eyes full of a gentle, pleading light, trying to pull me back from that distant, sorrowful place. "Do not think too harshly of him, Marietta. His methods are clumsy, I know, and his fear has made him a tyrant. But you must understand... he has wanted this, a child, an heir, for so very long. Even in his first marriage, it was a source of great, unspoken sorrow to him that the nursery remained empty. To finally have that hope, and then to have it threatened so terribly... it has made him lose his reason. His protectiveness is not for a title or a legacy; it is for a dream he had long ago given up on."

Her words painted a picture I had not considered, a picture of a man haunted not just by the ghost of a dead wife, but by the ghost of an unborn child. I could only manage a slow, weak nod, my mind struggling to reconcile this image of a wounded, hopeful man with the cold jailer he had become.

"He is wrong to keep Isabelle from you, I know," Lady Tamsin continued, giving my hand a firm, reassuring squeeze. "Her laughter is a cure, not a cause for alarm. I will speak with him. I will try to make him see reason. Give me a little time to persuade him. For now, you must rest, my dear. Rest and be strong, for the both of you."

I squeezed her hand in return, a flicker of gratitude in the vast emptiness.

Lady Tamsin's words, meant as a comfort, only highlighted the maddening, painful puzzle of it all. He was trying to save our child, and in doing so, he was slowly, methodically, and with the best of intentions, breaking my heart. How could the presence of one small, quiet child be a threat? What possible reason could he have for this sudden, cold-hearted cruelty?

The gilded cage of my bedchamber had become a true prison, and the one person in the world who could have offered me any real comfort had been locked out, her small, sad face a constant, agonizing presence on the other side of a door I was not permitted to open.

I did not know the truth. I did not know that in his mind, a terrible, tragic certainty had taken root. He did not see Isabelle as a comfort. He saw her as the source of my illness, the living, breathing embodiment of the emotional stress the doctor had warned against. He was not punishing me; he was protecting his heir, and in his twisted, fearful logic, that meant protecting me from the ghost of a past he had so profoundly, catastrophically misunderstood.

17

A Worsening Silence

Marietta

My prison was a beautiful one, all pale blue silks and gleaming silver furniture, but it was a prison nonetheless. In the week that followed Callum's decree, the four walls of my bedchamber became the entire world, a silent, gilded cage where I was left alone with my thoughts, my fears, and the tiny, secret life that was both the source of my deepest joy and the cause of my current torment.

The silence was the worst part. It was a thick, muffling thing, broken only by the deferential whispers of the maids who brought my meals, or the distant, mournful ticking of the grandfather clock in the hall. It was a silence designed for healing, for placid contemplation. But for me, it was a breeding ground for anxiety.

Separated from my daughter, my heart existed in a state of constant, low-grade ache. Every childish laugh I thought I heard from the gardens, every patter of small feet I imagined in the corridor, was a fresh twist of the knife. Isabelle was in this house, my beautiful, precious girl, and she was forbidden to me. She would be asking for me, wondering why the 'Aunt Marietta' who had been her constant companion had suddenly vanished. She would think I had abandoned her, just as I had been forced to do once before. The thought of her small, sad face, her confusion and her hurt, was a pain so profound it was a physical thing.

My stress, instead of abating in the prescribed quiet of my sickroom, began to fester. The quiet was not restful; it was a vacuum, and into that vacuum rushed all my fears. I was trapped, with nothing to do but lie in bed and contemplate the impossible, tangled web of my life. My mind would circle endlessly, a frantic, trapped bird, beating its wings against the bars of my gilded cage.

Callum's coldness. Isabelle's absence. My aunt's manipulations. My father's cruelty. The secret of my past and the secret of my present were two monumental weights pressing down on my soul, and in the lonely silence of my room, they threatened to crush me completely.

And as my emotional turmoil grew, my body, that treacherous and all-too-honest vessel, began to rebel. The mild nausea of the previous weeks returned with a vengeance, no longer a fleeting morning queasiness, but a constant, rolling sickness that made the thought of food a torment. The simple broths and jellies that were sent up from the kitchen would sit untouched on their silver trays, their scent alone enough to make my stomach clench. I grew weaker, the world outside my windows seeming to fade into a pale, watery thing.

Callum continued his scheduled, clinical visits. He would appear in my doorway twice a day, a tall, formidable figure, his face a mask of cool, unreadable concern. He would look at my untouched tray, at my pale, drawn face, and I would see the lines around his mouth tighten.

"You are not eating," he would state, his voice flat.

"I have no appetite," I would whisper, my gaze fixed on the silken canopy of the bed.

He would not press. He would not offer words of comfort. He would simply stand there for a long, silent moment, a statue of ducal disapproval, and then he would turn and leave, his footsteps echoing in the hallway. I knew what he was thinking. He saw my decline not as a symptom of my confinement, but as proof of it. Proof that my fragile, emotional nature was a danger to the child I carried.

I did not know then that his twisted logic had already found its scapegoat. I did not know that every pale, drawn look on my face, every untouched meal, was another piece of evidence in his mistaken, tragic prosecution of an innocent child. He saw my worsening condition and it only hardened his resolve, confirming in his fearful, father's heart that he had been right to separate me from the source of my "agitation." He was trying to save me, to save our child, but his methods were a slow, exquisite form of torture.

The true terror came one evening, a week into my confinement. I had been attempting to read, the book resting on my knees, the words a meaningless blur on the page. I shifted in the bed, and I felt it. A sudden, slight cramping deep in my belly, a low, ominous ache that was frighteningly familiar.

I froze, my blood turning to ice. I remembered the first, tearing pains of my labor with Isabelle, the agony that had ripped my world apart. A wave of pure, primal fear washed over me. *No. Not now. It is too soon.*

I pressed a trembling hand to my abdomen, as if I could physically hold the tiny life within me, protect it with my own will. I lay perfectly still, my breath held in a silent, desperate prayer. The cramping subsided, a dull, receding ache. But when I moved again, a cautious, terrified motion, I felt a slight, damp warmth between my legs.

A sound, a half-sob, half-scream, tore from my throat. My hands flew to the sheets, pulling them back. And I saw it. Against the pristine white linen, a single, terrifying spot of bright, crimson blood.

The world dissolved into a roaring, black-edged tunnel of pure panic. My baby. I was losing my baby. The thought was a physical blow, so devastating it knocked the air from my lungs. This precious, secret hope, this one, fragile chance at a future, was being torn from me.

I did not remember pulling the bell rope, but I must have, because moments later, the door to my chamber burst open. It was not a maid. It was Callum. He must have been in his study, just down the hall. He stood in the doorway, his face a mask of shock, his eyes wide as he took in the scene—me, half-risen in the bed, my face a mask of pure, unadulterated terror, my trembling hand pointing at the single, damning spot of blood on the sheets.

He was at my side in an instant. For the first time in weeks, the Duke of Ice

99

was gone, his cool, controlled façade shattered by a fear that mirrored my own.

"Marietta," he said, his voice a raw, ragged thing. He gripped my hand, his fingers a tight, grounding pressure around my own. "What is it? What has happened?"

"The baby," I sobbed, the words torn from me, a frantic, broken plea. "Callum, the baby... our baby."

The look on his face in that moment will be seared into my memory for all time. The raw, undisguised terror, the flicker of a pain so profound, so absolute, it was as if he himself had been dealt a mortal wound. I saw then, in that one, unguarded instant, that he was not the cold, unfeeling automaton I had believed him to be. He was a man. A father. And he was just as terrified as I was.

He did not release my hand. He held it, a lifeline in the storm of my panic, his knuckles white. "Jennings!" he roared, his voice a sound of raw, unfamiliar terror that echoed in the hall.

A footman appeared in the doorway, his eyes wide. "Your Grace?"

"Ride for Dr. Arbuthnot," Callum commanded, his voice sharp and cracking with strain. "Ride as if the devil himself is chasing you. Do you understand?"

"Yes, Your Grace!" The footman vanished.

He turned his panicked gaze to a maid who had appeared behind the footman. "You! Find Mrs. Finch. We need cool water, clean linens, smelling salts. Now!"

As the maid scurried away, my own aunt and a pale, distraught Lady Tamsin appeared in the doorway, their faces masks of worry.

"Callum, what is it?" Lady Tamsin cried, rushing forward.

"She is bleeding," he said, his voice a broken, ragged thing as he finally looked back at me, his eyes a reflection of my own terror. "God help us, she is bleeding."

A fresh wave of cramping seized me, a vicious, tearing pain that stole my breath and made my body shudder violently. The world dissolved into a blur of worried faces and hushed, frantic voices. I clung to his hand, the only solid thing in a universe that was splintering apart, my own terror a silent scream that had no sound.

The next few hours were a living nightmare, a blur of cool cloths on my forehead, of the bitter, metallic taste of a draught the doctor forced me to drink. I was propped up on a mountain of pillows, my legs elevated, my body a still, silent battleground where the fate of my child was being decided.

Through it all, Callum did not leave my side. He remained in the chair by my bed, a silent, formidable sentinel. He did not speak. He did not touch me again. But his presence, his solid, unwavering watchfulness, was a strange and unexpected comfort. In this, our moment of shared, profound terror, we were not adversaries. We were allies, united by a single, desperate hope.

Finally, after what felt like an eternity, the cramping eased. The bleeding, which had been blessedly slight, stopped completely. Dr. Arbuthnot, after a final, gentle examination, straightened up, his face tired but relieved.

"The danger, for now, has passed," he said, his voice a low, reassuring murmur. "The draught has done its work. But Your Grace," he said, his gaze fixing on me with a new, stern intensity, "I cannot be more clear. You are in a most delicate state. You must have absolute, complete, and unwavering rest. No visitors. No excitement. No emotional distress of any kind. Your very life, and the life of your child, may depend upon it."

He then turned to Callum, his expression grim. "Your Grace, it is my medical opinion that the Duchess's current regimen is insufficient. The stress she is under, whatever its source, is a direct and immediate threat to this pregnancy. It must be eliminated. Completely."

I watched as Callum listened to the doctor's words, his face a mask of stone. I saw the fear in his eyes slowly, chillingly, recede, replaced by a new, colder, and more absolute resolve. I saw the conclusion he was drawing, the terrible, logical leap his mind was making.

The doctor's words, meant to save us, had instead become my final, damning sentence.

He looked at me then, his gaze no longer that of a terrified, fellow parent. It was the cool, assessing gaze of the Duke once more. The fragile, momentary alliance forged in our shared fear, was over. He believed he had found the source of the stress that had nearly cost us our child.

And I knew, with a cold, hollow certainty that settled in the pit of my stomach, that his resolve to protect his heir, at any and all costs, had just hardened into a thing of pure, unyielding iron. He would eliminate the threat. And in his tragically mistaken mind, the threat had a name. And her name was Isabelle.

18

The Duke's Investigation

Callum

F ear is a cold and clarifying thing. In the endless, agonizing hours
I sat by my wife's bedside, listening to the shallow whisper of her
breath, my world had narrowed to a single, terrifying point: the
fragile, flickering life of my unborn child. The moment I had seen that single,
crimson spot on the white linen, the entire, complex machinery of my life—
my political ambitions, my ducal duties, my own wounded pride—had ground
to a halt. There was only the raw, primal terror of a man on the verge of losing
everything he had not even known he truly wanted.

I had held her hand, felt the cold, trembling fragility of her fingers in
mine, and in her panicked, tear-filled eyes, I had seen a reflection of my
own desperation. For a brief, timeless moment, we were not the Duke and
Duchess, not adversaries in a silent war. We were a man and a woman, a
father and a mother, united in a single, desperate prayer.

But the moment the immediate danger passed, the moment Dr. Arbuthnot's
steadying presence had filled the room, the fear had begun to cool, to harden,
crystallizing into a new and absolute resolve.

*"Emotional stress... a direct and immediate threat... It must be eliminated.
Completely."*

The doctor's words were a death knell, a verdict, and a command. And I, the Duke of Highmoor, was a man who knew how to act on a command. I was a man who knew how to eliminate a threat.

The source of her stress, the root of this near-catastrophe, was no longer a mystery to me. It was not the strain of her new life or the pressures of the title. It was the ghost she refused to relinquish. Her all-consuming grief for the poet, Julian Thorne. I had witnessed how her bizarrely intense affection for my aunt's ward, Isabelle, was a trigger for her emotional turmoil. That strange, obsessive bond was a symptom of the deeper sickness in her heart—a heart that was still bound to another man. That emotional instability was the direct threat to my heir.

I would not allow it to happen again.

The days following the scare were a study in absolute, unwavering control. I transformed Redwyck House into a fortress, a sanctuary dedicated to a single purpose: the protection of the Redwyck heir. Marietta was a sacred, fragile vessel, and I would be her unyielding guardian. She remained confined to her chambers, a command from Dr. Arbuthnot that I enforced with military precision.

Her diet was the first front in my campaign. I met with Mrs. Finch and the cook every morning, reviewing the day's menu with the grim focus of a general planning a siege. Nourishing broths, simple jellies, milk puddings— only the blandest, most fortifying foods were permitted. I forbade the serving of anything with a strong scent or rich flavor, recalling with a cold clarity her aversion to certain dishes in the weeks prior. At the time I had seen it as a sign of her secret grief; I now saw it as a physical manifestation of her delicate condition, a vulnerability I would not permit to be tested.

Dr. Arbuthnot attended her every other day. I was always present for his examinations, a silent, formidable sentinel in the corner of the sickroom. I would listen to his quiet questions, to her weak, whispered replies. I would observe as he checked her pulse, his expression a mask of professional neutrality. After, I would walk him to the door, my questions sharp and precise. Was her strength returning? Was her color improved? Was the child safe?

I was a constant, silent presence in her life. I did not offer her tenderness; the fragile bridge between us had been washed away by the tide of my own fear. I offered her something I believed to be far more valuable: my absolute, unwavering protection. She was quiet, listless, her eyes holding a deep, distant sorrow. I saw her grief not as a betrayal now, but as the very poison the doctor had warned against. And I, as her husband and the father of the child she carried, had a duty to administer the cure, no matter how painful.

But managing the symptoms was not enough. To truly eliminate the threat, to truly secure the peace of mind necessary for my wife to carry our child to term, I had to do more than just manage the present. I had to conquer the past. I had to understand the full story of Julian Thorne. I had to know the nature of his hold over her, the full extent of their connection. I had to neutralize his ghost, to ensure he could never reappear, in rumor or in fact, to upset the fragile balance of my wife's health and my heir's future.

It was with this cold, clear purpose that I summoned a man named Mr. Dawes to my study.

Dawes was not a man one found through polite society. He was a creature of the shadows, a former Bow Street Runner who now operated a private investigative service for a select, wealthy clientele. He was discreet, thorough, and utterly without scruple. He was precisely the man I needed.

He arrived on a rain-swept afternoon, a small, grey, unassuming man who seemed to blend into the shadows of my study. He stood before my desk, his hat in his hands, his pale eyes missing nothing.

"Your Grace," he said, his voice a low, gravelly thing.

I did not waste time with pleasantries. "I have a task for you, Mr. Dawes," I said, my voice the cool, formal instrument of business. "It is a matter of the utmost delicacy and requires absolute discretion. Is that understood?"

"Perfectly, Your Grace," he said.

I pushed a small, heavy purse of coins across the polished expanse of my desk. "This is your retainer. Your final payment will be commensurate with the thoroughness and the speed of your work."

He took the purse without a word, its weight a silent, satisfying thud in his palm.

"I need you to uncover everything there is to know about a man," I continued, my gaze fixed on his. "His name is Julian Thorne." I spelled it for him, the very sound of the name a bitter taste in my mouth. "He was a poet, active in London society approximately four years ago."

Dawes's expression did not change, but I saw a new, sharper level of attention in his gaze.

"I require a complete history," I said, my voice as cold and as hard as iron. "His parentage, his finances, his associations. Especially his female companions." I paused, letting the weight of my request settle. "He was involved in a scandal with a Miss Marietta Greystone. I need to know everything about that affair. When it began, how it was conducted, how it ended. I want to know if they maintained contact after the scandal broke. I want to know where he went when he fled the country."

My voice was a low, steady monotone, betraying none of the raw, burning jealousy that fueled my words. I was not a jealous husband seeking to expose a rival. I was a strategist, gathering intelligence on an enemy.

"And most importantly," I concluded, my gaze pinning him to the spot, "I need to know where he is now. I have reason to believe he may still be alive, despite rumors to the contrary. If he is, I want to know his location, his circumstances, his current state of mind. I want to know if he is a threat."

Dawes listened, his head tilted slightly. He was a vault, a perfect, silent repository for the dark and secret needs of men like me.

"It will be done, Your Grace," he said, his voice a quiet promise of efficiency.

"Discretion is paramount, Dawes," I reiterated, my voice a low warning. "No one is to know of your investigation. Not my staff, not my wife, not a soul. If so much as a whisper of this inquiry reaches the society pages, you will find that my displeasure is a far heavier thing than this purse."

"I understand the stakes, Your Grace," he said with a curt nod. He slipped the purse into his coat, and with it, the ghost of Julian Thorne. He bowed, and then he was gone, melting back into the rain-swept London afternoon.

I was left alone in the silent, shadowed study. I had set a dangerous machine in motion. I had unleashed a bloodhound on the trail of my wife's secret past. I knew that what he brought back might be a truth so painful, so devastating, it could shatter the last, fragile remnants of my marriage.

But the fear of the truth was nothing compared to the fear I now felt for my unborn child. I was a father, and a father's first duty is to protect. I would protect my heir from the ghosts of the past, even if it meant declaring a silent, secret war on the woman I had, in a moment of foolish, sunlit weakness, allowed myself to love. The die was cast. And I would see the game through to its bitter, necessary end.

19

A Mother's Bond

Marietta
My gilded prison grew more unbearable with each passing day. The days bled into one another, a monotonous and unchanging river of time. I would wake, take my breakfast from a tray, sit by the window, and watch the world outside move on without me. The silence, meant to be a healing balm, was a suffocating shroud. The rest, meant to restore my strength, only served to amplify the frantic, helpless turmoil of my own thoughts. In this static, silent world, only one thing was dynamic. One thing proved that time was not standing still.

Each morning, I would stand before the pier glass after my bath, and I would see it: the slow, inexorable rounding of my abdomen. It was the only new thing in my life, the only secret sign that the days were indeed passing. The slight curve was a quiet, constant companion in my endless solitude. I would watch Callum's gaze at dinner, a cool, analytical assessment that would sometimes linger for a fraction of a second on my waistline before flicking away. He said nothing, but his silent observation was a part of the monotonous ritual of our lives.

This quiet, physical change was my only clock, my only calendar, in a world that had otherwise stopped turning. I was a mother, separated from her child by nothing more than a few corridors and the unyielding, misguided will of my own husband. The injustice of it, the sheer, maddening cruelty of it, was a poison that seeped into my soul, leaving me weak and heartsick.

I would lie in my bed, the fine linen sheets feeling like a winding cloth, and I would listen. I would strain to hear the sound of Isabelle's laughter from the gardens, the distant patter of her feet in the hallway, any small sign that she was near. But the house was kept unnaturally quiet, the staff moving with a hushed reverence, as if I were already in mourning. The silence was a wall, and on the other side of it was my daughter.

Lady Tamsin was my only comfort, my only link to the world outside my chamber. She would visit me daily, her kind face a mask of worried sympathy, her cheerful chatter a brave but futile attempt to lift my spirits. She did not understand the true source of my sorrow, but she saw the pain in my eyes, and her gentle, maternal heart ached for me.

"He is a fool, that nephew of mine," she said one afternoon, her voice a low, indignant whisper as she plumped the pillows behind my back. "He means well, of course. He has always been fiercely protective. But he is a man, and like most men, he believes a problem can be solved by issuing a decree and locking the door. He does not understand that a woman's heart is not a fortress to be commanded."

I said nothing, merely offering her a weak, grateful smile. But her words planted a seed, a small, dangerous idea that began to take root in the barren soil of my despair. I could not continue like this. This passive acceptance, this slow, silent wasting away, was a betrayal of myself and of the child I carried. If my husband would not see reason, then I would have to find a way around him.

The opportunity came three weeks after the bleeding scare, on the day of Dr. Arbuthnot's regular visit. Three weeks. It had been an eternity of silent, gilded imprisonment. My body had healed; the doctor had pronounced me stable after the first week, but Callum's iron-willed regimen had not relaxed. I was a prisoner in my own chambers, and my soul was beginning to wither from the lack of fresh air and the constant, aching absence of my daughter.

My secret was also becoming more difficult to hide. At four months now, my pregnancy was no longer a secret known only to my heart. It was a gentle but undeniable curve to my abdomen, a new fullness in my breasts. The loose gowns and clever draping could only do so much. I felt as if my body was a walking declaration of the truth I was so desperate to conceal.

Dr. Arbuthnot finished his gentle examination, a kind, paternal smile on his face. He was a good man, a man who had kept his word, and he had become my only ally. Callum stood by the fireplace as always, a silent, formidable sentinel, his gaze fixed on the doctor, awaiting the verdict.

"Her Grace is progressing splendidly," the doctor announced, his voice cheerful. "The baby has a strong, steady heartbeat, and the Duchess's own strength has returned admirable. In fact," he added, turning his kind eyes to me, "I believe a bit of gentle activity is in order. A short, slow walk in the gardens each day, on a fine afternoon, would do you a world of good. The fresh air would be a fine tonic."

A surge of pure, unadulterated hope shot through me. The garden. Freedom. A chance.

"Absolutely not," Callum said, his voice a low, flat thing from across the room. It was not a suggestion; it was a decree. "The risk is too great. You were most clear, Doctor. No agitation."

Dr. Arbuthnot did not flinch from the ducal glare. "I was, Your Grace. And a gentle stroll amongst the roses is hardly a great agitation. It will lift Her Grace's spirits, which is just as important for her health, and the health of the child, as any amount of bed rest."

Callum's jaw tightened, but he could not argue with the voice of medical authority. I, however, saw my chance, the first small crack in the walls of my prison, and I seized it with a strength I did not know I possessed.

"I should like that very much, Doctor," I said, my voice quiet but firm, my gaze meeting my husband's across the room. It was not a request. It was a statement of intent. I would not endanger my baby for a selfish whim, but I would not remain a prisoner when my own doctor had granted me a reprieve.

Callum's expression was a mask of cold disapproval, but he said nothing more. The doctor had given the order.

Later that morning, he came to my chambers before his departure. He was leaving for a necessary political meeting in Westminster and would be gone for the entire day. He gave me a long, searching look, his grey eyes filled with that now-familiar mixture of concern and suspicion.

"You will rest today, Marietta," he said, his voice a quiet, unyielding command. "The doctor said a short walk. He did not say a marathon."

"I will be a perfect invalid," I promised, my voice a soft, demure thing that was a masterpiece of deception.

The moment the sound of his carriage wheels faded down the long drive, a new, frantic energy filled me. I rang for my maid. My plan was not a reckless act of defiance. It was a calculated risk, sanctioned by a physician. I would not endanger my child. But my other child... my daughter... the need to see her was a physical ache, a call on my soul I could no longer ignore. I chose a simple, loose-fitting morning gown, ignoring the maid's worried protests that His Grace preferred I remain in bed.

"His Grace is not here," I said, my voice quiet but firm, a flicker of the Duchess's authority returning to me. "And I find the air in this room has become... stale. I will sit in the sun room for an hour."

My legs were a little unsteady at first, my body weakened by days of inactivity, but every step I took towards freedom was a victory. I found Lady Tamsin in the sun room, just as I had hoped. She was arranging a vase of roses, her expression one of distracted sorrow. She looked up as I entered, her eyes widening in alarm.

"Marietta, my dear child! What are you doing out of bed? Callum will have my head!"

"Callum is in Westminster," I said, closing the glass door behind me, sealing us into a private, sunlit world. I walked to her, my heart pounding a frantic, desperate rhythm against my ribs. "And I cannot bear it a moment longer, Aunt. You must help me."

She saw the raw, desperate plea in my eyes, and her own kind face softened with an immediate, unwavering empathy. "Anything, my dear. What is it?"

"I need to see her," I whispered, the words a raw, painful confession. "Just for a moment. Please. The separation... it is making me ill, not well. I miss her so desperately, it is a physical pain."

Lady Tamsin's expression shifted from confusion to a dawning, profound understanding. She looked at my pale, tear-streaked face, at the desperate, almost manic intensity in my eyes, and she finally saw the truth that her nephew, in his logical, masculine blindness, could not. She did not know the secret, but she saw the love. She saw that my connection to Isabelle was not the casual fondness of a new aunt, but something deeper, something more powerful, something that was as essential to my well-being as the air I breathed.

"Oh, you poor, dear child," she murmured, her own eyes growing misty. She took my hands in hers, her grip a warm, comforting pressure. "Of course. Of course, you do. He is a fool, a blind, beautiful fool. He thinks he is protecting you, but he is caging you." She gave my hands a firm, conspiratorial squeeze. "Very well. But we must be clever. The servants are his eyes and ears. We cannot meet here."

A plan was quickly, quietly formed, a small, secret conspiracy of women against the well-meaning tyranny of a man. Lady Tamsin, it turned out, was a brilliant strategist in her own right.

"The old summerhouse," she declared, her eyes sparkling with a newfound excitement. "At the bottom of the west garden. It is quite secluded. No one ever goes there. I will tell Isabelle's governess that the child is to have her afternoon lesson *en plein air*. And you, my dear, will tell your maid that you require a short, slow walk in the garden for some fresh air, as prescribed by the doctor. I will ensure your maid is... distracted. Meet us there in one hour."

The hour that followed was the longest of my life. I sat by my window, watching the clock on the mantelpiece, every tick of the second hand a slow, torturous beat. I was filled with a mixture of wild, exhilarating hope and a profound, gut-wrenching terror. I was defying my husband. I was actively plotting against him, in his own house. If we were discovered, his anger, his sense of betrayal, would be a terrible thing to behold. But the thought of seeing my daughter, of holding her in my arms, was a pull so powerful it eclipsed all fear.

Following my aunt's instructions, I made my slow, careful way down the servants' staircase and out into the gardens. The fresh, warm air was a balm on my skin, the scent of roses and cut grass a heady perfume. I kept to the secluded paths, my heart pounding with every rustle of the leaves, every

112

distant sound from the house.

The summerhouse was a small, charming folly of white-painted wood, half-hidden by a cascade of climbing roses. I slipped inside, the air cool and smelling of dust and dried flowers. And then, a moment later, she was there.

Isabelle entered, her hand in her governess's, her small face lighting up with a pure, unrestrained joy the moment she saw me.

"Aunt Marietta!"

She ran to me, and I knelt, catching her in my arms, holding her close against my chest. The feel of her, the scent of her, the sheer, miraculous reality of her, was a wave of pure, unadulterated bliss. All the pain, all the fear, all the loneliness of the past week melted away, replaced by this one, perfect, stolen moment.

Lady Tamsin had given the governess a task that would conveniently occupy her at the far end of the garden for the next half an hour. We were alone.

"I missed you," Isabelle whispered, her small arms tight around my neck.

"I missed you too, my darling," I whispered back, my voice thick with unshed tears. "More than you will ever know."

We sat together on the dusty wooden bench. As I settled her on my lap, her small hand came to rest on the gentle, firm curve of my abdomen, which was now undeniable beneath my loose-fitting gown. Her touch was innocent, a simple, childish curiosity.

"Your tummy is round, Aunt Marietta," she stated, her green eyes, *my* green eyes, wide with observation. She patted the swell gently.

Before I could find the words to answer, Lady Tamsin, who had been watching us with a fond smile, spoke. "That is because your Aunt Marietta has a new baby growing in there, my love," she said softly. "A little cousin for you to play with."

Isabelle's face lit up with a look of pure, uncomplicated delight. "A baby sister?"

"Or a brother," I managed to say, my voice a tight, aching thing.

Isabelle's gaze turned from my stomach to my face, her expression one of profound, childish seriousness. "Was I in your tummy too?" she asked.

The question was a clean, sharp blow to my heart. It was the most natural question in the world, and the most impossible one for me to answer. I could only stare at her, my throat closing over a thousand unspoken truths. *Yes, my love. Yes, you were. You grew right here, under my heart.*

Lady Tamsin, ever-gracious and quick, stepped smoothly into the silence. She sat beside Isabelle and stroked her dark curls. "No, my sweet girl," she said, her voice a gentle, loving melody. "You grew in *my* tummy. You were my special baby."

It was a kind lie, a necessary fiction to protect a child's heart, but for me, it was a fresh severing, another layer of separation from my own daughter. I watched as Isabelle accepted this, turning to give Lady Tamsin a hug, and I felt a grief so profound it was a physical emptiness.

Isabelle, satisfied, turned her attention back to me and chattered on, telling me of a new doll, of a story she had read, of a particularly interesting beetle she had found under a stone. And I listened, hanging on her every word as if they were the most profound pronouncements ever uttered. I was memorizing her, hoarding these precious, fleeting moments, storing them up for the long, lonely days I knew were to come.

I braided a small, lopsided crown for her from the wildflowers that grew by the door. She placed it on her head and declared herself the Queen of the Summerhouse, and I, her loyal subject. We laughed, our shared joy a bright, beautiful, and deeply secret thing.

In that small, dusty summerhouse, I was not the Duchess. I was not a prisoner. I was a mother, playing with her child. And the taste of that simple, forbidden freedom was the sweetest, most painful thing I have ever known.

All too soon, I saw the governess making her way back up the path. Our time was over.

The severing, this time, was a quiet, gentle agony. I knelt before her, my hands on her small shoulders.

"I have to go now, my love," I said softly.

Her face, which had been so bright and animated, crumpled with a sudden, childish sorrow. "But you will come back tomorrow?" she asked, her lower lip trembling.

The question was a knife in my heart. "I will try," I lied, the word a bitter taste in my mouth. "I will always, always try."

I gave her one last, fierce hug, pressing a kiss to the top of her head, and then I watched as the governess led her away, her small, skipping figure disappearing behind a hedge of roses.

I remained in the summerhouse for a long time, alone with the scent of dust and the ghost of her laughter. The joy of our secret meeting was a warm, glowing ember in my chest. But it was surrounded by the cold, encroaching chill of reality. This could not last. These stolen moments were a temporary, dangerous solution.

I had defied my husband. I had tasted a freedom I knew I could not live without. And as I made my way back to the main house, back to my gilded cage, a new, more dangerous resolve began to form in my heart. I could not live like this, a secret mother, a guest in my own daughter's life. Something had to change. Something had to break. And I knew, with a dawning, terrifying certainty, that it would have to be me.

20

The Investigator's Report

Callum

The waiting was a refined form of torture. For ten days, I existed in a state of suspended animation, my public life a mask of ducal calm, my private thoughts a relentless, circling storm of suspicion. Every knock on my study door, every delivery of the daily post, sent a jolt of anxious, angry energy through me. I was waiting for Dawes. I was waiting for the truth.

My wife, meanwhile, was a study in contradictions. Her physical health, under the strict regimen I had imposed, seemed to be improving. The color was returning to her cheeks, her appetite was stronger, and the profound, bone-deep weariness seemed to be lifting. Dr. Arbuthnot, on his weekly visit, had pronounced himself cautiously optimistic.

"The immediate danger to the pregnancy," he had declared, his expression relieved, "seems to have passed. Her Grace is recovering her strength splendidly."

I had seen the proof with my own eyes. On the rare occasions she rose from her bed to sit by the window, I could see the undeniable, healthy swell of her abdomen beneath the loose silk of her robes. The sight of her growing belly, a tangible promise of the heir to come, was a source of profound, quiet reassurance. The child was growing. The child was strong. My methods, however harsh, were working.

His words should have brought me a profound sense of relief. They did not. They only sharpened the edges of my suspicion. Her physical health was improving, yes, but the source of her original distress—the ghost that haunted her—remained. My orders for her complete confinement were working; by shielding her from the agitations of the outside world, her body was healing. To my logical, analytical mind, the correlation was clear. I had identified her obsessive grief for the poet as the poison, and by isolating her from any reminders of her past, I was saving the patient.

Yet, she was no happier. The sorrow in her eyes had not abated; it had simply gone deeper, hiding behind a new, more resilient façade of quiet, serene grace. She was more distant than ever, a beautiful, polite stranger who shared my name and my house. Our conversations were brief, formal exchanges about household matters or the weather, masterpieces of polite evasion. The woman I had held at the inn, the woman whose laughter had filled the gardens at Ravenswood, was gone, and this pale, sad ghost was all that remained.

She had begun to defy me, in her own quiet, subtle way. I was not a fool. I knew that she was leaving her chambers when I was away from the house. I would return from a day of meetings in Westminster to find a book in her sitting room that had not been there that morning, or the faint, fresh scent of rosewater on the air, a sign that she had been in the gardens. I saw the signs, the small rebellions. I knew that my aunt, in her soft-hearted, sentimental way, was likely aiding and abetting her.

I allowed it. Her small acts of defiance were a risk, yes, but they were also a sign of a returning strength, a strength the child she carried desperately needed. I would permit her these minor transgressions, these stolen moments of air and movement. But on one point, I was unyielding: the child, Isabelle, was to be kept from her sickroom.

The image was burned into my mind: Marietta, her face radiant, lifting the small girl into her arms, and then the sudden, terrifying collapse. The doctor's words about the danger of any "shocks or upsets" echoed in my head.

In my mind, the two events were now one. I could not shake the image of the child's small, solid body pressing against my wife's abdomen at the very moment she fainted. The thought of that weight, however slight, resting on the place where my own child was so fragilely growing, filled me with a cold, irrational fury. It was a simple, physical threat, an unnecessary risk I would not permit. Her affection for the girl was a dangerous liability. My heir's life depended on my vigilance.

And so I waited, trapped in a cold, silent war with a wife I no longer knew, my only hope for clarity a small, grey, unassuming man who moved through the shadows of the city.

He arrived on a Thursday, just as a grim, autumnal rain had begun to fall, streaking the tall windows of my study. He appeared at my door as if summoned by the weather, a creature of grey skies and damp secrets. He was, as always, impeccably discreet, his presence barely registering with the footman who announced him.

"Mr. Dawes is here, Your Grace."

"Send him in," I said, my voice a calm, even thing that betrayed none of the frantic, anxious energy that had seized me at the sound of his name.

He entered, his hat in his hands, his pale eyes missing nothing. He laid a slim, leather-bound folio on the polished expanse of my desk. It landed with a soft, final thud, the sound of a verdict being delivered.

"The report, Your Grace," he said, his voice a low, gravelly thing.

"You were successful?" I asked, my gaze fixed on the folio. It was a Pandora's box, and I both craved and dreaded to open it.

"As Your Grace commanded," he said with a curt nod. "The subject was... forthcoming in his history. A man of passion leaves a wide trail. Debts, letters, angry husbands. It is all there."

My hand hovered over the folio. "And his current location?"

"That is in the report as well, Your Grace," he said, his expression unchanging. "The final page."

I dismissed him with a gesture, and he melted from the room as silently as he had come. I was left alone with the truth. Or, at least, with Dawes's version of it.

I poured myself a brandy, the amber liquid a stark, vivid color against the grey, rain-swept afternoon. I did not drink it. I simply held the heavy crystal tumbler, its coolness a small, inadequate anchor in the storm of my own thoughts. I sat down in the heavy leather chair behind my desk and, with a hand that was not quite steady, I opened the report.

The first few pages were a dry, factual account of a life lived in reckless pursuit of pleasure and poetry. Julian Thorne. Born the second son of a minor baron, a respectable but impoverished lineage. Educated at Cambridge, where he was noted more for his romantic entanglements and gambling debts than for his scholarship. He had come to London five years ago, a handsome, charming, and utterly penniless poet, and had quickly made a name for himself in the city's literary salons.

Dawes's report was meticulous. It detailed Thorne's finances, a sordid history of loans taken and never repaid, of promissory notes signed and defaulted upon. It listed his patrons, a collection of wealthy, bored society women who were charmed by his pretty words and his even prettier face.

And then, I turned the page, and I saw her name.

Miss Marietta Greystone.

My breath caught in my throat. Seeing her name there, in this sordid, clinical report, felt like a profanity, a desecration. Dawes had been thorough. He had interviewed former servants, disgruntled creditors, jilted lovers. He had pieced together the entire, shameful affair.

It had begun at a summer house party. A whirlwind of stolen moments in moonlit gardens, of secret meetings in borrowed rooms. He had written her sonnets. He had sworn he would leave his long-suffering wife. He had promised her a life of passion and poetry in Italy. She, a naive, romantic girl of nineteen, had believed him.

I read the account, my knuckles turning white where I gripped the pages. A cold, bitter fury rose in me. A fury at this man, this shameless, predatory scoundrel who had targeted a young, innocent girl and filled her head with his cheap, secondhand lies. He had not loved her. He had seen her as a prize, a beautiful, well-bred conquest, another testament to his own irresistible charm.

And she, in her innocence, had fallen. The scandal had broken, just as Dawes's sources had recounted. Thorne's wife had discovered the affair. The whispers had begun. And Thorne, my wife's great and tragic love, had revealed himself for the coward he truly was. He had retreated to the country with his wife, leaving Marietta to face the inferno alone.

The report confirmed it all. The ruin. The disgrace. The public condemnation. It was all there, in stark, black-and-white ink. I felt a surge of something I had not expected: a fierce, protective pity for the young, foolish girl my wife had once been. She had been a victim, not a schemer. A casualty of a cruel man and a crueler society.

But my pity was quickly eclipsed by a colder, more immediate question. This was the past. What of the present? The report confirmed that Thorne had fled to the continent to escape his debts and the scandal. But where was he now? Was he still writing to her? Was he the ghost that still held her heart?

My gaze fell to the final lines on the page. Dawes had tracked Thorne's movements after he left England. A sad, pathetic trajectory of a man spiraling into obscurity. Paris, then Rome, then a small, forgotten village in the south of France. His meager funds had run out. His patrons had forgotten him. His pretty words had lost their currency.

I held my breath, my entire being focused on the thin, crisp sheet of paper in my hand. My gaze swept over the dry, factual account of Thorne's final years, searching for the one, crucial piece of information I needed. The answer to the question that had been tormenting me for weeks. The key that would unlock the secret of my wife's sorrow.

I reached the end of the page. The report, it seemed, was concluded. But then I saw it. Tucked at the bottom, almost as an afterthought, was a final, single sentence.

My fingers trembled as I turned the page to reveal the final, most crucial piece of information.

21

The Ghost of a Rival

Callum

I turned the page. The paper was crisp and cool beneath my trembling fingers, a stark contrast to the hot, frantic pounding of my own blood. The final page of the report was mostly empty, containing only a few lines of Dawes's neat, economical script. It was a summary, a final, damning conclusion to the life of a man who had become my phantom rival, my unseen enemy.

I read the words, and the world, which had already been a fractured and unstable thing, simply ceased to exist.

Julian Thorne died in a pauper's hospital in Marseilles, France, two years ago. The cause of death was listed as consumption. He was buried in an unmarked grave.

I read the sentence once. Then again. And then a third time, but the words would not cohere into a meaning I could accept. They were a foreign language, a code I could not decipher. My mind, a cold, logical engine, had seized, its gears grinding to a halt against a fact so absolute, so impossible, it could not be processed.

Dead.

The man was dead.

He had not lingered. He had not written her letters. He had not been a living, breathing ghost haunting the edges of our marriage. He had been a real ghost all along. A collection of dust and bone in an unmarked patch of French soil.

For a long, silent moment, I simply stared at the words, a roaring, white-hot silence filling my ears. The brandy glass, still held in my hand, slipped from my numb fingers and crashed to the floor, the sound a sharp, splintering explosion in the quiet of my study. I did not flinch. I did not move. I was a statue, frozen in a moment of absolute, world-altering revelation.

And then, the ice that had encased my heart for weeks did not just crack; it shattered. It shattered into a million sharp, glittering pieces, and in its place, a wave of pure, unadulterated horror washed over me.

I had been wrong.

It was not a simple error in judgment. It was a profound, catastrophic, and monstrous miscalculation. My entire theory, the intricate, logical fortress of suspicion I had so carefully constructed, was built on a foundation of absolute, unequivocal falsehood.

There was no living rival. There was no active conspiracy. There was no secret lover her family had lied about. There was only a dead poet and a grief I had so profoundly, so tragically, misunderstood.

I sank back into my chair, the report still clutched in my hand, my body trembling with the aftershock of the revelation. A cold sweat broke out on my brow. I felt a wave of nausea so intense it was as if I myself had been poisoned.

I saw it all with a new, horrifying clarity. The past few weeks replayed in my mind, not as a series of betrayals, but as a litany of my own inexcusable cruelties. I saw Marietta's pale, tear-streaked face, her eyes wide with a fear and a sorrow I had dismissed as guilt. I heard her desperate, broken words— *"I lost... someone precious..."*—and I felt the echo of her grief, a grief I had twisted into an accusation.

I saw my own face in the dim light of the carriage on our journey home from Fitzgibbon estate, a mask of cold, jealous fury. I heard my own voice, a whip of sarcasm and suspicion, as I spat the words at her: *"Am I to be nothing more than a name and a title to you, a convenience to shield you while your heart belongs to a ghost?"*

The memory of my own words was a physical blow. I had accused her of mourning a ghost, and I had been right, but in the most ignorant and cruel way imaginable. She *had* been weeping for a ghost, for a past she could not reclaim, and I, in my blind, arrogant pride, had seen it not as a tragedy, but as a betrayal of *me*.

My actions since her collapse... dear God. My mind reeled with the sheer, breathtaking scale of my own monstrousness. I had confined her to her room, a prisoner in her own home. I had treated her not as my wife, but as a fragile, untrustworthy vessel. I had overseen her care with a clinical, cold precision, my concern not for her, but for the heir she carried.

And Isabelle. The child.

The full weight of my cruelty towards an innocent little girl descended upon me. I had banished her from Marietta's presence. I had looked at her, a small, beautiful, and utterly blameless child, and I had seen her as a threat, a symbol of my wife's imagined infidelity. I had caused her pain, her confusion. I had made her believe she was the cause of her new aunt's illness and seclusion.

I had been acting like a tyrant. A monster. For years, a cold rage had simmered within me every time I heard the whispers, the stories that painted me as a cruel, unfeeling beast. I had told myself they were lies, the filth spun by gossips. But now, in the horrifying clarity of this moment, I saw the truth. I had taken their vicious caricature and, through my own blind, wounded pride, I had made it real. I had been so consumed by my own past, by the ghost of Violetta's betrayal, that I had projected her sins onto another woman, a woman whose only crime was a sorrow I was too blind and too wounded to understand.

A low, wounded sound, a half-groan, half-sob, was torn from my throat. I dropped my head into my hands, the rough paper of the report crinkling against my temple. The shame was a living thing, a vile, coiling creature in my gut. I had been so certain, so logical, so damningly, absolutely sure of my own conclusions. I had built a case, and I had prosecuted it, and I had found her guilty. And the verdict, the entire trial, had been a lie.

I had been profoundly, catastrophically wrong.

After a long while, the first, violent wave of self-loathing receded, leaving in its place a cold, clear, and even more terrifying confusion. I lifted my head, my gaze falling once more on the final, damning sentence of the report.

Julian Thorne died... two years ago.

The fact was a stone, a hard and immovable object in the center of my shattered worldview. The man was dead. He had been dead long before I ever met Marietta. He could not be the source of her present-day terror. He could not be the reason she had flinched from my touch in the dusty inn room. He could not be the reason she had looked at me with such profound, hopeless sorrow when I had confessed that I cared for her.

The ghost I had been fighting was a phantom of my own making. Which meant the ghost she was fighting, the true source of her secret sorrow, was something else entirely. Something I did not begin to comprehend.

If the man is dead, what is she so terrified of?

The question echoed in the silent, shadowed study. It was the only question that mattered. She was not a schemer. She was not a liar. She was a woman in the grip of a profound and terrible fear, a fear so powerful it had made her ill, a fear she believed would destroy me if she spoke its name.

"You would hate me for it." Her words from that night in the dining room returned to me, no longer sounding like a defiance, but like a desperate, terrified plea. *"It would destroy you!"*

What secret could be so monstrous? What past transgression could possibly carry such a devastating power in the present?

My mind, free now from the fog of my own jealous suspicions, began to work again, to turn over the pieces, to look at the puzzle from a new angle. Her ruin. The affair. The public disgrace. The timeline of it all was laid bare before me, but the central piece of the puzzle, the source of her present-day terror, was still missing.

I rose from my chair, my movements stiff, my mind reeling with the sheer, catastrophic weight of my own misjudgment. I had to know. I could not live another moment in this labyrinth of secrets and misunderstandings. The time for silent, watchful suspicion was over. The time for cold, hard logic had failed me. There was only one path left.

I had to go to her. I had to lay the truth, the one, irrefutable truth I now possessed, at her feet. And I had to ask her the real question, the one that had been hiding beneath all my anger and my pain.

I left the study, the crumpled report still in my hand, a testament to my own blindness, and walked towards my wife's chambers. I was no longer an adversary. I was no longer a judge. I was just a man, a man who had been terribly, horribly wrong, and who was now, finally, ready to listen.

22

The Real Confrontation

Marietta

I was a prisoner awaiting a sentence that never came. The days following my bleeding scare were a blur of enforced rest and quiet, suffocating solitude. Callum, true to his word, had eliminated all sources of "agitation" from my life with a ruthless efficiency. The world outside my bedchamber ceased to exist. There were no visitors, no letters, no newspapers. And most painfully, there was no Isabelle.

My physical strength slowly returned, but my spirit withered. I was trapped in a beautiful, silent prison, haunted by the ghost of my daughter's laughter and the cold, watchful presence of a husband who had become my jailer. He was a constant, silent sentinel, his concern a clinical, suffocating thing that felt less like care and more like surveillance. He saw me as a fragile, volatile vessel, a problem to be managed for the sake of the precious heir I carried. He did not see me at all.

I had given up trying to understand the source of his new, colder suspicion. I had resigned myself to this lonely, silent existence, my only hope the tiny, secret life that grew within me, a life I protected with a fierce, desperate silence of my own. We were two strangers, bound by a child, separated by a universe of secrets.

It was a grey, listless afternoon, the sky outside the color of old pewter, when he came to me. I was sitting in the armchair by the fire, a book of poetry lying unread in my lap. I had not heard him approach, and I started when the door to my chambers opened.

He stood on the threshold, and the man I saw was not the cold, formidable Duke who had been my warden for the past week. The anger, the suspicion, the icy control—it was all gone. In its place was a man who looked utterly, devastatingly lost. His face was pale and drawn, his eyes shadowed with a profound and weary exhaustion. He looked like a man who had been to war and had returned bearing the invisible, heavy wounds of a battle lost.

He held a crumpled piece of paper in his hand, his knuckles white where he gripped it. He did not speak. He simply walked towards me, his steps slow, almost hesitant, and came to a stop before my chair. He looked at me, and for the first time in what felt like an eternity, I saw not a judge, not an adversary, but the man I had held in the chapel, a man in the grip of a deep and desperate pain.

My heart, which had been a dull, listless thing, began to beat a slow, wary rhythm. I did not know this man, this new, broken version of my husband. I did not know what he wanted.

"Callum?" I whispered, my voice a breath of concern in the quiet room. "What is it? What is wrong?"

"I have been a fool," he said, his voice a low, rough thing, stripped of all its ducal authority. It was the voice of a man confessing a mortal sin.

He held out the crumpled paper to me. "I believe you should read this."

I took it, my fingers trembling slightly. It was a page from a report, the script neat and clinical. My eyes scanned the words, and my breath caught in a sharp, painful gasp.

Julian Thorne died in a pauper's hospital in Marseilles, France, two years ago. The cause of death was listed as consumption. He was buried in an unmarked grave.

I stared at the words, a wave of pure, unadulterated shock washing over me. Dead. Julian, my first love, the man whose beautiful, ruinous lies had set the course of my entire life, was dead. He had been dead for two years. The grief I had thought I would feel, the sharp pang of loss for the boy I had once loved, did not come. There was only a profound and weary sadness, a quiet, final closing of a chapter I had not realized was still open.

But my own quiet shock was nothing compared to the realization that crashed over me a moment later. Callum. He had investigated Julian. He had hired someone to unearth the sordid, shameful details of my past. The paper in my hand began to tremble, a violent, rattling tremor that I could not control. I looked up at him, my lips shaking, the words a raw, disbelieving whisper.

"You... you investigated me?"

The question hung in the air between us, a stark and painful accusation. A hot, furious wave of indignation rose in me, but it was extinguished as quickly as it came. I looked up at his face, and I saw not the triumph of a prosecutor who had found his proof, but the raw, naked shame of a man who had been terribly, horribly wrong.

"I know what you have been hiding," he said, his voice a raw whisper. "I know why you have been so... distant. So sad. I believed... I allowed my own past, my own ghosts, to poison my mind. I believed you were grieving for a man who was still alive. That your heart belonged to another. I saw a conspiracy where there was only sorrow. I have been a blind, arrogant, and unforgivable fool."

The confession, so raw and so complete, left me speechless. He had been jealous. The coldness, the suspicion, the cruelty of the past weeks—it had not been a rejection of me. It had been born of his own wounded, twisted, and profoundly mistaken fear of losing me to a rival. The realization was a staggering, heartbreaking thing.

"And I know," he continued, his voice breaking, "that I have been a monster. I have treated you like a prisoner. I have caused you pain when all you have ever shown me is a strength I do not deserve. I have been so wrong, Marietta. About everything."

He sank to his knees before me, a gesture of such profound, humble supplication that it shattered the last of my defenses. He took my hands in his, his grip a desperate, pleading thing. "I am so sorry," he whispered, his forehead resting against our joined hands. "Forgive me."

Tears streamed down my own face, silent tears of a sorrow and a relief so profound they had no name. He was not a monster. He was a man, a proud, wounded man who had been so terrified of being betrayed again that he had become a tyrant. And he was here, on his knees, begging for my forgiveness.

I threaded my fingers through his, a silent, willing acceptance. "There is nothing to forgive," I whispered, my voice thick with my own tears.

He looked up then, his grey eyes, those eyes I had once thought so cold, now filled with a desperate, aching confusion.

"But I still do not understand," he said, his voice a raw plea for the truth. "I was wrong. The ghost I was fighting was a phantom of my own making. But you... you are still fighting yours. I see it in your eyes. I feel it in your silence."

He reached out, his hand coming up to gently, reverently, cup my jaw. "I know he is gone, Marietta. The report proves it. So you must tell me. You must help me understand."

He held my gaze, his own filled with a desperate, weary, and all-encompassing need to finally, truly, see me.

"If he is gone," he whispered, his voice the sound of a man baring his very soul, "what is the secret that you are so afraid of?"

23

The Weight of the Truth

Marietta

H is question hung in the air between us, a quiet, desperate plea that echoed in the silent, firelit room. *If he is gone, what is the secret that you are so afraid of?*

The moment had come. The moment I had both craved and dreaded since the day I first set eyes on Isabelle at Ravenswood. There were no more shadows to hide in, no more misunderstandings to serve as a shield. He had dismantled his own fortress of suspicion and had come to me, not as a Duke, not as a judge, but as a man, his heart bare, his confusion a raw and open wound. He had offered me the truth, and now he was asking for my own in return.

I looked down at his face, at this proud, formidable man kneeling at my feet, his grey eyes filled with a pain and a vulnerability that mirrored my own. I saw the man who had protected me from falling books, who had defended my honor against vicious gossips, who had held me through a storm and confessed that he cared. And I saw, with a clarity that was both terrifying and liberating, that he deserved more than the half-truths and evasions I had been feeding him. He deserved the whole, ugly, and devastating truth.

To speak it would be to risk everything. His disgust, his rejection, the utter annihilation of the fragile, burgeoning love between us. But to remain silent now, in the face of his raw, humble honesty, would be a betrayal of a different, more profound kind. It would be a confession that I did not trust him, that I did not believe him capable of understanding, of empathy, of forgiveness. And as I looked into his eyes, I knew, with a sudden, soul-deep certainty, that I could not bear to be that kind of coward. Not anymore.

I took a deep, shuddering breath, a breath that felt as if it were the first I had taken in years. I gently withdrew my hands from his and used them to cup his face, my thumbs stroking the sharp, elegant line of his jaw.

"You were right," I whispered, my voice a raw, trembling thing. "I have been hiding a secret from you. A ghost. But it is not the ghost of a man."

I saw the flicker of confusion in his eyes deepen. I rose from my chair and helped him to his feet, leading him to the settee by the fire. We sat, the space between us no longer a chasm, but a fragile, shared ground. I did not release his hand. I clung to it, a lifeline in the storm I was about to unleash.

"The ruin that has followed my name for four years," I began, my gaze fixed on the dancing flames of the fire, "it is not just a story, Callum. Not just a scandal of a foolish girl's affair. It had... a consequence."

I felt his hand stiffen in mine, but he said nothing. He simply waited, his silence an invitation, a promise to listen.

"The poet, Julian Thorne... he was my first love. I was a foolish, romantic girl, and he was a man of beautiful words and easy lies. He promised me a future he had no intention of providing. And I, in my innocence, gave him everything. My heart, my honor... and my body."

The words were a quiet, shameful confession in the firelit room. I risked a glance at him. His face was a mask of stone, but his eyes were fixed on me, his gaze intense, unwavering.

"I discovered I was with child a month after the scandal broke," I continued, my voice dropping to a near-whisper. "He had already abandoned me, retreated to the country with his wife, leaving me to face the inferno alone. I was terrified. I was nineteen years old, and my entire world had collapsed. I told my father."

The memory of that night, of my father's face, not of sympathy, but of cold, hard fury, rose up before me. "He did not see me as his daughter. He saw me as a disgrace, a stain on the family name that had to be erased. A plan was made. I was sent away, to a remote, empty summer manor on the coast of Northumberland. I was a prisoner, attended only by a midwife and a handful of trusted servants who were sworn to secrecy."

I could feel the story pouring out of me now, a flood of suppressed pain and memory. "The world was told I had suffered a nervous collapse and had been sent to the continent to recover. It was a lie. I spent the next seven months in that house, alone, watching my body change, feeling my baby grow, my heart a constant, warring mixture of love and of terror. I loved the child I carried with a fierceness that was the only real thing in my life. But I was so terribly, terribly afraid of what would happen when she was born."

My voice broke on a sob, and his hand tightened around mine, a silent, steadying pressure.

"The night she was born," I whispered, the memory as vivid and as raw as if it were yesterday, "was a storm of pain and of fear. I was in labor for twelve hours. I was forbidden from crying out, for fear a passing traveler might hear. And then... she was here. She was the most beautiful thing I had ever seen. She was perfect. She had a full head of dark, curling hair, and a tiny, crescent-shaped birthmark on her forehead."

Tears were streaming down my face now, but I did not stop. I had to tell him. All of it.

"The midwife laid her on my chest. I held her for... for less than a minute. It was the only minute of my entire life that I have ever felt a joy so pure it was like a piece of heaven. And then my father came. He took her from my arms. She was crying for me, and he ripped her away. He told me I had forfeited all rights to her, that she was a disgrace that would be erased. He told me I would never see her again."

The raw, ragged pain in my own voice was a shocking thing. "They took her away that night. I did not know where. I was sent to a convent in France the following week. A month later, a letter arrived from my aunt. She informed me, in the coldest, most clinical terms, that the child had been sickly and had not survived. She wrote that it was a mercy."

132

I felt his hand clench around mine, a convulsive, furious movement, but I could not stop. The words were pouring out now, a flood of poison I had held inside for years.

"For three years, I lived as a ghost, my life a barren, empty thing. I mourned my daughter. I grieved for a tiny, unmarked grave I could never visit. My heart was not in a grave with a dead lover, Callum. It was in a secret grave of its own, with a child I believed was lost to me forever."

I finally dared to look at him. His face was a mask of pure, stunned shock. His skin was pale beneath his tan, his mouth a grim, tight line. He looked as if I had physically struck him.

It was now or never. I had to tell him all of it.

"And my body..." I whispered, my gaze dropping to my lap, the shame a hot, burning thing in my cheeks. "It was... changed. The birth left marks. Faint, silvery lines on my stomach. The proof of what I had done, what had been done to me. I have hidden them from everyone, terrified you would see them and know my ruin was not just a story, but a physical truth."

I took a shuddering breath. "And then," I said, my voice dropping to a near-whisper, "you and I were married."

I paused, gathering the last of my courage to explain the misunderstanding that had almost destroyed us. I looked up, my eyes pleading with him to understand. "That night, in the unused sitting room... when you followed me from the library... I wanted you, Callum. More than I had allowed myself to admit. But when we were on the chaise, and your hand moved to my stomach... I... I flinched. I pulled away. Not from you. Never from you. I was afraid. I was terrified you would feel the marks in the darkness, that you would see my shame and be disgusted by me. I ruined that moment because I was a coward."

The dawning, horrified understanding in his eyes was so profound it was almost a physical thing. He was not just learning my secret; he was finally, truly understanding the source of my rejection, the root of the coldness that had defined the beginning of our marriage.

"I thought," I continued, my voice trembling, "that my fear had destroyed any chance we might have had. I believed that night had sealed our fate, that we would be strangers forever. I thought all the ghosts belonged to the past... and then we went to Ravenswood."

The last piece of the puzzle clicked into place.

"Your aunt, in her kindness, introduced us to her ward," I said, my voice trembling. "A small, beautiful girl with a cascade of dark curls. A girl who was just shy of her fourth year. A girl with my own green eyes."

He made a small, choked sound, but I could not stop. The truth, once unleashed, had to run its course.

"I knew," I whispered, my gaze locked with his. "The moment I saw her, a part of my soul recognized her. And then I saw it. A small, faint birthmark on her forehead, shaped like a crescent moon. It was my daughter, Callum. The child my father had stolen from me. Her name is Isabelle."

My hand, as if with a will of its own, came up to clutch my pregnant belly, a desperate, protective gesture over the new life I carried, a shield against the ghosts of the past. I took a shuddering breath, the words tumbling out now in a raw, broken confession.

"I never meant to deceive you. As you know, I never wanted this marriage— I never wanted any marriage. My aunt forced me back into society. Our meeting... it was an accident. And I swear to you, Callum, I did not know she was alive. They told me she had died. For three years, I mourned her. For three years, I believed my child was dead. I did not know until the moment I walked into your aunt's drawing room."

My palm cups my belly—protective, desperate—guarding the tiny heart growing within. Tears streamed down my face as I finally gave voice to the fear that had been poisoning my joy.

"And this child..." I whispered, my voice breaking on a sob. "This baby... I know you want him. I know you will be a wonderful father. And a part of me is so profoundly, deeply happy to be carrying the child of a man I have come to... to love. But I am so afraid, Callum. I am terrified of being pregnant again. I am terrified of the joy, because the last time I felt it, it was stolen from me. I am so afraid that this child, too, will be taken away."

The final word fell into the silence of the room, a single, devastating stone dropped into a deep, still pond. The story was told. The secret, in all its ugly, heartbreaking, and terrified truth, was out.

I watched him, my heart in my throat, my entire being braced for his reaction. I expected a surge of cold, ducal fury at the deception. I expected a recoil of disgust.

He did none of those things. He simply stared at me, his grey eyes wide with a mixture of shock, of horror, and of something else, something so profound and so unexpected it shattered the last of my fear. It was empathy. A deep, raw, and all-encompassing empathy.

He did not see Lady Ruin. He did not see a liar or a schemer. He saw a woman who had endured an agony he could not even begin to comprehend. He saw a mother whose child had been stolen from her.

He did not drop my hand. Instead, he used it to draw me closer, his other hand coming to rest, firm and protective, over mine on my pregnant belly. He looked me directly in the eye, his own gaze a fierce, unwavering vow.

"Listen to me, Marietta," he said, his voice a low, rough thing, thick with an emotion I could not name. "No one will ever take this child from you. Not your father. Not anyone. This child is a Redwyck. He is *ours*. And I will burn the world to the ground before I let anyone harm you, or our children, ever again."

He held my gaze for a moment longer, sealing his vow, before his expression hardened, the empathy twisting into a cold, lethal fury directed at the source of my pain. He lifted my hand, his movements slow, almost reverent, and pressed his lips to my knuckles in a gesture of such profound, humble respect that a fresh wave of tears choked me.

He finally spoke, his voice turning into a quiet, dangerous hiss.

"And your father," he said, "will answer for this."

24

The Duke's Reckoning

Callum

The world had tilted on its axis before. It had tilted when I learned of Violetta's betrayal, and again when I had read the investigator's report confirming Julian Thorne's death. But this, this was not a tilting. This was a complete and utter inversion, a tearing of the very fabric of reality. I was in free fall, plummeting through a void of disbelief, and the only thing anchoring me to the world was the small, trembling hand I held in my own.

Her name is Isabelle.

The words echoed in the silent, firelit room, a quiet, simple statement of fact that had the force of a physical blow. I stared at my wife, at the pale, tear-streaked face of this woman I had thought I was beginning to know, and I saw a stranger. Not a stranger in the way I had before, not a creature of secrets and deception, but a woman who had endured a tragedy so profound, so monstrous, it was beyond the realm of my comprehension.

My mind, a cold, logical engine, tried to reject it. It was impossible. A melodrama. A fiction spun from grief and a series of impossible coincidences. But my heart, that treacherous, newly awakened organ, knew the truth. I saw it in the raw, unadulterated pain in her eyes. I saw it in the way every piece of the maddening puzzle of her behavior now clicked into place with a devastating, perfect clarity.

Her collapse at Ravenswood upon first seeing the child. Her profound, inexplicable grief at leaving. Her terror when my aunt had suggested she might be pregnant. Her constant, weary sadness. It was not for a lost lover. It was for a lost child. A child who was not lost at all, but who had been living under my own family's protection, a constant, unknowable, and agonizingly close presence.

The first emotion to rise from the ashes of my shock was a wave of pure, white-hot fury. It was a rage more profound than any I had ever known, a volcanic, primal anger that was so intense it was a physical sickness. But for the first time in my life, that fury was not directed at a woman who had betrayed me.

It was not directed at Marietta. My God, not at her. She was not a perpetrator; she was the primary victim in a conspiracy of cruelty so profound it defied belief.

No, my rage was for them. For her father, the Viscount Greystone, a man I now saw as a monster cloaked in the robes of aristocratic honor. I pictured his cold, implacable face, and I felt a surge of violent, murderous intent. To rip a newborn child from its mother's arms, to condemn his own daughter to a life of silent, secret grief, to perform an act of such breathtaking, soul-destroying cruelty in the name of *family honor...* it was a perversion of the very word.

And her aunt. Lady Tiverton. The cold, calculating creature who had pushed her niece back onto the society chessboard, knowing full well the secret she carried. Who had watched Marietta's pain, her sorrow, and had seen it as nothing more than a strategic inconvenience to be managed.

They had not just ruined her reputation; they had hollowed out her soul. They had stolen her child, stolen her past, and left her a ghost, a walking wound, and then they had thrown her at me, hoping my title, my name, would be a sufficient, gilded cage to contain her grief.

"Your father," I had hissed, *the words torn from me, "will answer for this."* And I meant it. I meant it with every fiber of my being.

But hot on the heels of that rage came a second, more personal, and far more devastating emotion: a wave of shame so profound it was like a physical drowning.

My own blindness. My own breathtaking, arrogant, and unforgivable cruelty.

I saw myself as if from a great height, a small, foolish man, puffed up with his own wounded pride. I saw myself at the Fitzgibbons' supper, my mind poisoned with suspicion, twisting the whispers of gossips into a damning, false narrative. I saw myself in the carriage, my words a whip of jealous fury, accusing her of mourning a ghost when she was, in fact, the one who was being haunted.

I saw myself in this very house, a tyrant in my own home. I remembered the cold, clinical way I had treated her after her bleeding scare, my concern not for her, but for the heir she carried. I saw myself banishing Isabelle from her presence, my face a mask of stern, ducal authority, believing I was protecting my child, when in fact I was torturing my wife, twisting the knife in her deepest, most sacred wound.

I had seen her pain, and I had named it jealousy. I had seen her terror, and I had named it guilt. I had been so consumed by the ghost of my own past, by the memory of Violetta's betrayal, that I had been utterly, damnably blind to the reality of hers.

A low, guttural sound, a half-groan of pure, unadulterated self-loathing, was torn from my throat. I had believed myself to be her adversary. I had believed I was uncovering her secrets, protecting my house from her deception. The irony was a bitter, scalding thing. The only deception in this house had been my own. I had deceived myself.

I looked at my wife, at this woman who had endured so much, who had borne the weight of this impossible secret in a silence so profound it had nearly shattered her. I saw not the fragile, volatile creature I had believed her to be, but a woman of a strength so immense it was humbling. She had protected her child's secret, her child's future, even at the cost of her own happiness, her own peace of mind. She had endured my coldness, my suspicion, my cruelty, and she had not broken.

The last of my anger, the last of my pride, simply dissolved, washed away by a tide of overwhelming, all-encompassing empathy. I did not just feel pity for her. I felt a profound, aching respect. A sense of awe.

I lifted her hand to my lips again, but this time, it was not a gesture of respect. It was an act of pure, humble supplication. I was not a Duke. I was not a husband. I was just a man, on his knees, in the presence of a courage he could not begin to comprehend.

"Forgive me," I whispered, my voice a raw, broken thing against her skin. "Marietta, forgive me. For my blindness. For my cruelty. For every cold word, every suspicious glance. I did not know. My God, I did not know."

She was weeping freely now, but they were not the silent, desperate tears of before. They were tears of release, of a burden finally shared. She threaded her fingers through mine, her grip a fragile, trusting thing.

"There is nothing to forgive," she whispered back, her voice thick with her own tears. "How could you have known? It was a secret I did not believe could ever be told."

I rose to my feet and pulled her into my arms, holding her not with the desperate, angry passion of before, but with a new, reverent tenderness. She was so fragile, her body trembling in my embrace. I held her, my hand stroking her hair, my own heart a painful, aching knot in my chest. I had been given a gift, a second chance, a woman of a strength and a grace I did not deserve. And I had nearly destroyed her.

We stood there for a long time, in the flickering candlelight, two broken, wounded souls, clinging to each other in the wreckage of our own making. The secrets were finally out, the ghosts laid bare. The war was over.

But as I held my weeping wife in my arms, I knew that the true battle, the battle to heal, to rebuild, to find a way to forge a real marriage from the ashes of so many lies and so much pain, had only just begun. And I, who had been so terribly, horribly wrong, would spend the rest of my life trying to be worthy of the woman who had, against all odds, offered me her trust.

25

A Desperate Flight

Marietta

I had confessed. In the quiet, firelit sanctuary of his study, I had taken the shattered, shameful pieces of my past and laid them at my husband's feet. I had unburdened my soul of the secret that had been my constant, silent companion for four long years, and I had waited for the world to end.

But it had not ended. He had not recoiled in disgust. He had not turned from me in cold, ducal fury. He had looked at me with an empathy so profound, so absolute, it had felt like a physical grace. He had taken my hands, and in his touch, in his raw, broken apology for his own blindness, I had felt the first, fragile, and miraculous stirrings of a future I had never dared to imagine. For a few, precious, stolen moments, I was not his Duchess, and he was not my Duke. We were just a man and a woman, two broken souls finding a strange, beautiful solace in the wreckage of our shared secrets.

But the moment, like all beautiful things, was fragile. He had risen to his feet, pulling me into a gentle, protective embrace, a promise of a new beginning. And then I saw it. As he held me, his gaze shifted over my shoulder, towards the fireplace, and the look of tender, aching empathy in his eyes was slowly, chillingly, replaced by something else.

It was a cold, hard glint, a flicker of the formidable, dangerous man I knew him to be. The Duke of Highmoor had returned. And his face, when he looked down at me a moment later, was a mask of calm, controlled, and utterly terrifying fury.

But the fury, I realized with a fresh wave of cold terror, was not for me.

"Your father," he had said, his voice a quiet, lethal hiss, "will answer for this."

The words, meant as a promise of protection, a declaration of his allegiance to me, struck me not as a comfort, but as a threat. I saw in his eyes not just a husband's anger, but the cold, calculating wrath of a political titan. I saw the Duke of Highmoor, a man who moved pieces on the great chessboard of England, preparing to unleash his full, formidable power.

And in that moment, the fragile, beautiful hope that had just been born in my heart withered and died. I had unleashed a storm, a hurricane of ducal rage, and I had no idea where, or upon whom, it would break.

He saw the look of pure, unadulterated terror on my face, and he mistook its source. He thought I was afraid for myself, for the consequences of my confession. He did not understand that my fear was not for me, but for them. For Lady Tamsin, whose quiet, happy life was about to be engulfed in a scandal of epic proportions. And most of all, for Isabelle. My daughter. My innocent, blameless child, who was about to become a pawn in a war between two powerful, unyielding men.

"Marietta," he said, his voice a low, soothing rumble, but his eyes were still hard as grey stones. "Do not be afraid. I will handle this. I will protect you. I will protect the child."

The child. He meant the one I carried, the Redwyck heir. But what of my other child? My heart hammered against my ribs, a frantic, terrified rhythm. As if reading my thoughts, his gaze softened for a fraction of a second, but his words remained as hard as iron.

"And as for Isabelle," he continued, his voice dropping to a low, determined tone that chilled me to the bone, "her future will be secured. I will see to it personally. For the sake of my aunt, and for your own peace of mind, the girl's connection to your past will be severed completely. To the world, she will remain my aunt's daughter, and nothing more. No one will ever associate her with you, or with your ruin. You will be safe from it."

His words, meant as a promise of absolute protection, a vow to erase the stain of my past, struck me as a sentence of a second, more final, abandonment. He was offering to protect me by legally and socially severing me from my own daughter forever.

And the most terrible, most heartbreaking part of it all was that I understood. Through the blinding fog of my own agony, I could see the cold, hard, ducal logic of his decision. He was not being cruel for the sake of cruelty. He was a man protecting his house, his name, and the future of the legitimate heir I now carried. He was protecting his family from a scandal whose true, devastating nature he could not even begin to guess. I could not fault his reasoning. I could not even call him selfish. His decision was the most sensible, the most logical course of action. It was the decision a Duke *must* make.

And that understanding was a far greater pain than simple anger could ever be. He was not a monster to be hated. He was a man of honor, acting honorably, and in doing so, he was methodically, logically, and with the best of intentions, annihilating my soul.

For his ducal honor demanded that he see not a child to be loved, but a wrong to be righted; an injustice to be avenged by erasing all trace of the connection between us. He would not be a father in this; he would be a Duke, a warrior, and his battle would be fought on the public stage, with my daughter's life as the battlefield.

The thought was a physical blow. A wave of dizziness, swift and absolute, washed over me. I swayed in his arms, the room tilting, the firelight blurring into a hazy, indistinct smear.

"I need... I need a moment," I whispered, pulling away from him, my hands held out as if to ward off his terrifying, protective rage. "Please. I need to be alone. To think."

He let me go, his expression one of pained confusion. He believed my distress was the natural, emotional aftermath of my confession. He did not see that it was a new and more potent terror, a fear of the very man who was promising me his protection.

The moment the heavy study door closed behind him, the last of my strength deserted me. My legs gave way, and I sank to my knees on the thick Aubusson carpet, a low, wounded sound tearing from my throat. I was not safe. My daughter was not safe. His promise of protection was a death sentence for her future. He would wrap her in the Redwyck name, legitimize her, and in doing so, he would brand her forever with the scandal of my past. He would destroy her to save her.

Panic, cold and absolute, seized me. I had to stop him. But how? He was a force of nature, a Duke whose will was law. Words would not sway him. Reason would not reach him. He was a man consumed by his own rigid code of honor, a code that was about to annihilate my child's life.

I scrambled to my feet, my mind a frantic whirlwind. I could not stay here. I could not face him again. To be in this house, under his roof, felt like being trapped in a cage with a beautiful, well-intentioned, and utterly deadly lion. I needed help. I needed an ally.

I fled. I did not run, but I moved with a speed that was a frantic, desperate prayer, my hand pressed against my abdomen, a shield for the other child whose life I was now risking. My silk slippers whispered on the marble floors of the long, silent corridors. The portraits of his ancestors stared down at me with cold, judging eyes, their painted faces seeming to condemn the hysterical, ruined woman who had brought such chaos into their orderly world. I took a back staircase, my breath coming in short, painful gasps, my legs trembling with the effort. Every shadow was a threat, every creak of the floorboards the sound of his approaching footsteps.

There was only one place to go. One person who might understand.

I did not ring for a maid. I simply moved through the silent, shadowed corridors, a ghost fleeing from one part of the mausoleum to another. My silk slippers whispered on the marble floors as I made my way to the west wing, to the guest chambers where Lady Tamsin and Isabelle were staying.

I found her in the private sitting room that adjoined her bedchamber. She was seated by the fire, a piece of embroidery in her lap. She looked up as I burst into the room, her kind, familiar face lighting up with a smile of pure, uncomplicated pleasure. "Marietta, my dear! I was just thinking of you."

Her smile died as she saw my face, as she took in my wild, haunted eyes, my trembling posture. "My dear child," she said, her voice sharp with a sudden alarm, "what is it? What has happened?"

She rushed to my side, her arms going around me in a warm, comforting embrace. And at her touch, at the first, simple act of unquestioning kindness I had received all day, the last of my fragile composure shattered.

I collapsed against her, my body wracked with a storm of silent, wracking sobs. She led me to the settee, murmuring soothing, nonsensical words, her hand stroking my hair as if I were a lost and terrified child. She pressed a glass of sherry into my hands, but I could not drink. I could only weep, a tide of fear and of grief and of a profound, soul-deep terror for the future I had just unleashed.

"He knows," I finally managed to choke out, my voice a broken, unrecognizable thing.

Lady Tamsin's face was a mask of confusion. "He knows what, my love? Who knows?"

"Callum," I sobbed. "He knows everything."

"Everything about what?" she asked, her voice gentle but firm as she tried to make sense of my hysterics. "Marietta, you must calm yourself and speak plainly. What secret are you speaking of?"

But I could not be plain. The full story was a monstrous, tangled thing I did not have the strength to tell. In a broken, frantic, and often incoherent torrent of words, I tried to explain the unexplainable. Not the whole story, not the beginning, but the end.

"Callum," I sobbed, the words torn from me. "He is going to ruin everything!"

Lady Tamsin gripped my shoulders, her kind face a mask of profound confusion. "Ruin what, Marietta? You must speak sense, child. What has happened?"

"My confession," I wept, my hands clutching at her sleeves. "I told him a secret from my past, and now... now he speaks of my father, of honor... he means to go to war, Aunt Tamsin! He means to bring the whole, ugly, shameful story out into the light!"

She stared at me, trying to piece together the frantic fragments. "A secret? From your time on the continent?" she pressed gently. "Marietta, whatever this disgrace was, Callum is your husband. He would not expose you to further shame."

"You do not understand!" I cried, my voice rising in a new wave of panic. "It is not me he seeks to protect! It is his own honor! And Isabelle... oh, God, Aunt Tamsin, what will happen to Isabelle?"

At the mention of the child's name, a new, deeper layer of confusion clouded her features. "Isabelle?" she asked, her voice sharp with a dawning alarm. "What has that sweet child to do with your past sorrows? Marietta, what is this about?"

I looked at her, at this kind, loving woman who had cherished my daughter as her own, and the weight of the full truth finally became too much to bear in silence. The dam of my control, which had held for four long years, finally, catastrophically, broke.

"Because she is mine," I sobbed, the words torn from the very depths of my soul. "She is not just a ward. She is my daughter. My child. The one they took from me."

The world seemed to stop. The air in the quiet, sunlit room grew thick and heavy. I watched as the color drained from Lady Tamsin's face, her expression transforming from gentle confusion to a look of pure, unadulterated shock. Her hands, which had been gripping my arms, fell away as if she had been burned.

"Your... daughter?" she whispered, the words a breath of disbelief.

"Yes," I wept, the full, ugly story pouring out of me now. "My father took her from me at birth. They told me she had died. I did not know she was alive until the moment I saw her at Ravenswood. And Callum knows. He knows she is my child, and he is going to start a war with my father that will place her, her name, her entire future, at the very center of a catastrophic scandal."

She stared at me, her kind eyes wide with a dawning, horrified understanding. She was not looking at the Duchess of Highmoor. She was looking at a terrified young mother, and she was finally, truly, seeing the full, devastating shape of the secret I had been carrying. She knew her nephew. She knew

145

the formidable, unyielding force of his will, the cold, ruthless precision with which he pursued a goal. And she understood, as I did, that his ducal rage, unleashed in the name of justice, would be a devastating, unstoppable force that would destroy the very child he sought to protect.

"Oh, my dear child," she whispered, her hands gripping my arms with a new urgency. "We must go to him. Together. Whatever this secret is, whatever shame you believe you carry, he is your husband. He will listen to reason. He will listen to *me*."

Her words, so full of a sensible, hopeful logic, only served to heighten my own terror. She did not understand. She could not possibly understand the stakes.

"He will not listen to me," I cried, my voice rising in a new wave of panic. "He believes he is protecting me, but he is going to destroy my daughter's life. Her name, her future... it will all be consumed by the scandal."

The stress of the day, the emotional cataclysm of my confession, the frantic, terrifying flight through the cold corridors of the house, it was all too much. My body, already in a delicate, fragile state, finally began to surrender.

"He will bring the whole ugly story to light, and she will be ruined, she will be..." My words broke off, a sharp, sudden gasp tearing from my throat. A familiar, vicious cramp seized me deep in my belly, a terrifying echo of the night I had nearly lost this child. "Argh..." The sound was a low, wounded thing. My hands flew to my abdomen, clutching the swell of my stomach as I doubled over.

Lady Tamsin's face was a mask of pure, white-hot terror. "Marietta, are you in pain?"

"I'm... fine," I tried to insist, but another wave of pain, sharper this time, stole my breath. The room, with its bright, cheerful colors, began to tilt and spin. The impending catastrophe, the collision of my two worlds, was no longer a fear. It was a physical reality, tearing me apart from the inside out.

"Marietta!" she cried, her voice a sharp, piercing sound.

I felt myself falling, a helpless, dead weight, into a familiar, welcoming darkness. My last conscious thought was not of myself, not of my husband, but of the two precious, fragile lives that were now hanging in the balance.

The daughter I had just found, and the child I was now, once again, in danger of losing. The storm I had unleashed was no longer a thing of rage and of words. It had become a thing of flesh and of blood. And its first casualty was me.

26

A Husband's Pursuit

Callum

The silence that descended upon my study was a living, breathing entity. It was filled with the ghost of her, the echo of her broken, whispered confession. I stood there, frozen, in the center of the room, my mind a maelstrom of shock, of fury, and of a dawning, terrible understanding.

Isabelle. Her daughter. The words were a relentless, chaotic mantra, a drumbeat of disbelief against the inside of my skull. It was a truth so monumental, so utterly outside the realm of what I had considered possible, that my mind could not yet fully grasp its implications.

My first coherent thought was not of anger, but of a profound, primal fear. I had seen the raw, naked terror in her eyes as I spoke of her father. I had mistaken it for the simple, emotional aftermath of her confession. I had not understood that my vow to protect her had sounded, to her ears, like a declaration of war.

I had to go to her. I had to make her understand that she was safe, that my anger was not for her. I strode from the study and into the dining room, where a bowl of fruit still sat on the sideboard. I took a single ripe peach, its soft, fragrant skin a small, inadequate peace offering, and made my way to her wing of the house.

I knocked softly on her door. "Marietta?" There was no answer.

A prickle of unease tightened the muscles in my neck. I opened the door. The room was empty. A book lay open on the chaise longue, its pages fluttering in the draft. She was gone.

"Anna!" I called, my voice sharper than I intended. Her maid appeared from the adjoining dressing room, her eyes wide.

"Where is the Duchess?" I demanded.

"I... I do not know, Your Grace," the girl stammered. "I thought she was resting."

My panic began to sharpen into a cold, hard dread. She was carrying my child. Her pregnancy was fragile. She had collapsed only weeks ago from emotional distress. My voice, when I finally found it, was not the controlled command of a Duke, but the raw, furious roar of a husband pushed past his limit.

"Search the drawing rooms. The library. Find her. Now."

The maid scurried away. I paced her chambers, the scent of her lavender perfume a torment.

"Jennings!" I bellowed, my voice echoing in the hall, causing the butler to appear in the doorway with eyes wide with shock.

"Find out where the Duchess is," I commanded, my voice sharp and cracking with a strain I did not recognize. "Search every room. Now."

"Yes, Your Grace!" The butler vanished.

I turned my furious gaze to a maid who had appeared behind him. "You! Go back to her chambers. See if she has left a note. Any indication of where she might have gone."

I strode back into the grand hall, my fist connecting with a heavy oak console table, the crack of the impact echoing like a gunshot in the cavernous space. Jennings, my butler, appeared as if summoned by the violence, his face a mask of shock.

"Where is she?" I roared, the sound raw and unfamiliar in my own ears. It was an impossible question, a demand born of pure panic.

Jennings paled. "Your Grace, we are looking..."

"Then look harder!" I thundered. "I want every damned room in this house turned upside down. Find her. Do you understand me? Find her now!"

The floor seemed to tilt. She had vanished. In her delicate condition, to be wandering alone... My mind raced, grasping for any possibility. Where does a hunted animal flee? To its den. To safety.

And in this entire, sprawling mausoleum, there was only one source of unconditional comfort. *My Aunt.*

The realization was a fresh wave of terror. The guest wing was on the far side of the house, a journey of long, drafty corridors and multiple staircases. For a woman in her condition, a woman who had been ordered to complete bed rest, such an exertion... it was madness. She was risking everything.

I did not walk. I ran.

The journey down the long, silent corridors of my own home was the most agonizing of my life. The portraits of my ancestors stared down at me with cold, judging eyes. The marble floors, usually a testament to my family's power, now seemed to stretch into an infinite, mocking distance. I was the master of this house, yet I was pursuing my own terrified wife through its halls, a stranger in my own kingdom.

I reached the archway that led to the west guest wing. The corridor beyond was lit by a single, soft lamp. I saw a maid hurry out of the sitting room, her face pale with alarm. And then, blocking the doorway, was my aunt.

She stood on the threshold, a small, bird-like figure in a dress of sober grey silk. But the familiar, warm affection was gone from her eyes. In its place was a look of cool, protective steel, an expression I had not seen on her face since I was a boy of ten and had been caught tormenting the stable cats. She was not my aunt. She was a lioness, guarding her cub. And I was the threat.

"Aunt," I said, my voice a breathless, urgent thing. "Is she here? Is she safe?"

"She is here," my aunt said, her voice a quiet, chilling thing that was a perfect mirror of my own ducal frost. "She is safe from the world. She is not, I fear, safe from you."

She did not move. She simply stood there, blocking my path, her small frame an immovable object.

"Let me see her," I demanded, my own voice taking on a hard, desperate edge. "I need to speak with her. To explain."

"You will do no such thing," she said, her voice unwavering. "You have done quite enough for one day, it would seem." She looked at me then, and the disappointment in her eyes was a physical blow, a judgment more damning than any shout. "I have just sent a footman for Dr. Arbuthnot. She collapsed the moment she arrived."

The world seemed to tilt. The ornate patterns on the wallpaper swam before my eyes. *Collapsed.* The word was a death knell. My greatest fear, the fear that had driven my every tyrannical action, had come to pass. My actions, my words, my rage, had endangered my wife and my child.

"Is she... is the baby...?" I could not finish the sentence. The words were a thick, choking lump in my throat.

"We do not yet know," my aunt said, and the coldness of her tone was a punishment, a deliberate twisting of the knife. "The doctor will determine that. But what I do know, Callum, is what I saw. I saw a terrified, desperate young woman burst into my room, half-mad with fear, collapse on my floor, sobbing your name. She was fleeing from *you*."

She took a step forward, and for the first time in my adult life, I felt a flicker of the childish fear I had once had for this formidable woman.

"I do not know the whole story," she continued, her voice a low, cutting whisper. "But I know that you, in your pride and your anger, have done something to terrify a woman who is already carrying a burden of sorrow that would crush a lesser soul. You have taken her fragile state, a state that requires the utmost care and tenderness, and you have thrown your ducal rage at it. You have endangered your wife and your child, Callum. Your own flesh and blood."

Every word was a perfectly aimed arrow, striking at the heart of my own raw, bleeding guilt. She was right. She was absolutely, damningly right.

"Now, you will listen to me," she said, her voice leaving no room for argument. "You will not enter this wing. You will not send her notes. You will not disturb her in any way. You will go back to your own rooms, and you will wait. You will wait until the doctor has seen her, until she is calm, until she is safe. And you will wait until *I* deem it safe for you to see her again. Am I understood?"

I, the Duke of Highmoor, a man whose commands shaped the course of the nation, could only nod, a single, mute, and humble admission of my own catastrophic failure. I was powerless. I had been stripped of my title, my authority, my very identity, and reduced to nothing more than a frightened, foolish man, standing in the corridor of his own home.

"Good," she said, her expression softening for a fraction of a second with a flicker of the pity she might show to a wayward, foolish boy. But it was gone as quickly as it came, replaced by that same protective, lioness glare.

She closed the door to the sitting room, the sound a quiet, definitive thud that echoed in the silent hall.

I was left alone in the corridor, humbled and powerless, staring at the closed door that separated me from my wife, my child, and the wreckage of my own making. I had tried to be a protector, and I had become the monster. And now, all I could do was wait.

The wait was a fresh form of torture. I did not return to my study. I remained there, in the west wing corridor, a silent, helpless sentinel. I paced the length of the Aubusson runner, the silence of the house pressing in on me, broken only by the frantic, panicked beating of my own heart. Every creak of the floorboards from behind the closed door, every hushed murmur of voices, sent a fresh jolt of terror through me.

After what felt like an eternity, the door opened. Dr. Arbuthnot emerged, his medical bag in his hand, his kind face etched with a weary professionalism. I was before him in an instant, my own face a mask of raw, desperate inquiry.

"The Duchess is resting," the doctor said, his voice a low, calming murmur before I could even speak. "We have given her a mild sedative. The immediate crisis has passed."

"The baby?" I asked, my voice a raw, broken thing. "Was there... was there any bleeding?" The memory of the single, crimson spot on the white linen was a searing image in my mind.

Dr. Arbuthnot shook his head, and I felt a wave of relief so profound it almost buckled my knees. "No, Your Grace. There was no bleeding this time.

The cramping was severe, but it appears to have been brought on entirely by a profound emotional shock. Her body reacted to the distress of her mind."

He looked at me then, his gaze direct and serious, no longer the physician addressing a Duke, but a man addressing a husband.

"Your Grace, I must be clear with you," he said, his voice firm. "The Duchess is now well past sixteen weeks. Physically, this should be the most stable period of her pregnancy. The womb is strong, the child well-established. Under normal circumstances, the risk of a miscarriage would be greatly diminished."

He paused, letting the weight of his next words settle. "But these are not normal circumstances. The primary threat to this pregnancy is not a physical weakness. It is stress. The Duchess's emotional state is exceedingly fragile. An episode like the one she has just endured places an enormous strain on her system. If she is subjected to another such shock..." He did not need to finish the sentence.

I understood. The threat was not a fall or a fever. The threat was in her mind, in her heart.

"She must be kept in a state of absolute tranquility," the doctor concluded, his voice a final, unyielding command. "No difficult conversations. No emotional upsets. Her peace of mind is not a luxury, Your Grace. It is a medical necessity. The survival of your heir depends upon it."

I gave a single, curt nod, the doctor's words a set of ironclad orders being branded onto my very soul. He left, and I was once again alone in the silent corridor. But the helpless, frightened man of a few hours ago was gone. In his place, the Duke had returned, armed now with a new, cold, and absolute purpose.

I knew the source of her stress. I knew the ghost that haunted her. And I knew, with a certainty that settled in my bones like a deep and bitter frost, that it was my duty, as a husband and as a father, to eliminate it completely.

The guilt was a fire in my gut, but the fear was a colder, sharper thing. For the first time, I understood what it meant to be truly powerless. All my authority, my title, my will—they were not just useless, they were the very weapons that had brought us to this precipice.

There was no enemy to conquer, no rival to defeat. The monster I had to cage was myself. My duty, then, was no longer a matter of pride or lineage, but of survival. Their survival. I had been their jailer, their tormentor. Now, I would be their shield. I would protect them, even if it meant protecting them from me.

27

The Stillness of a Beating Heart

Marietta

I drifted in a grey, timeless twilight of exhaustion and laudanum-laced sleep for what felt like an eternity. The world was a distant, muffled thing, its sharp edges softened by the doctor's prescription and my own body's desperate need for rest. I was vaguely aware of hushed voices, of the gentle, repeated touch of a cool cloth on my forehead, of the soft, comforting presence of Lady Tamsin, who seemed to be a constant, unwavering sentinel at my bedside. She was an anchor of quiet kindness in a turbulent, formless sea.

The first time I truly awoke, the room was steeped in the deep shadows of late evening. The laudanum had receded, leaving behind a dull ache in my limbs and a profound, hollow soreness deep in my belly. The memory of the cramping, of that vicious, tearing pain, returned with a jolt of pure terror. My hands, moving with a frantic, clumsy haste, flew to my abdomen. I pressed against the gentle swell, my entire being focused on the space within, searching for a sign, a flutter, a confirmation that the tiny life I carried had weathered the storm.

"He is well, my dear." Lady Tamsin's voice, soft as a whisper, came from the chair by the hearth. "The doctor has been. The baby is strong. The

155

cramping has passed. You are both safe. Now, you must only rest."

The relief was so profound, so absolute, it felt like a physical loosening of every muscle in my body. The baby was safe. My son was safe. Lady Tamsin did not speak of Callum, and I was too weary, too grateful for the simple fact of my child's survival, to ask. I allowed the tide of exhaustion to pull me back under, my hands still spread protectively over my womb.

The next day, the sun was a pale, watery thing against the windowpane. I felt stronger, the deep weariness replaced by a fragile calm. Lady Tamsin helped me sit up against a mountain of pillows, a tray with weak tea and a piece of dry toast placed before me. It was then that I noticed them. On a table across the room stood an enormous, extravagant bouquet of white roses, their scent filling the quiet room. They were so purely white they were almost severe, a perfect reflection of the man I knew had sent them.

In the three days I was a prisoner in my aunt-in-law's guest bed, there had been no angry letters, no furious demands to see me, no sign of the ducal rage I had so feared. There was only a profound and unnerving silence, punctuated by the arrival of these flowers each morning. The card, written in a stark, masculine hand, said only: *"Forgive me. C."*

The gesture was so unlike the man I thought I knew, so full of a quiet, humble remorse, that it confused me more than his anger ever could have. The war I had anticipated had not materialized. In its place was this... this silent, aching truce. It was a stillness that was not peaceful, but fraught with the tension of a held breath. What was he thinking? What had he decided? My mind, with nothing else to occupy it, turned these questions over and over, polishing them like stones of worry until they were smooth and heavy in my thoughts.

Dr. Arbuthnot came in the late morning. His examination was brief and gentle. He listened for a long time with his conical tube before straightening up with a reassuring smile.

"A strong, steady heartbeat, Your Grace," he said. "As robust as one could hope for. The danger has passed. But I must insist on at least another day of complete bed rest."

I could only nod, a wave of gratitude so profound it brought tears to my eyes.

The doctor left, but the silence he left behind was filled with new questions. There was still no sign of Callum, only his flowers. And more painfully, no sign of Isabelle. I imagined her in another part of this house, her small face full of confusion, wondering where her 'Aunt Marietta' had gone. The thought was a fresh, sharp ache.

That night, the loneliness was a physical presence in the room. I lay in the vast, unfamiliar bed, a single candle flickering on the nightstand, and I wept. They were not the violent, frantic sobs of before, but silent, weary tears for the impossible, tangled knot my life had come to. Tears for the daughter I could not see, and for the husband whose silent apology I could not begin to comprehend.

On the fourth day, I was finally strong enough to sit up in a chair by the window, a cup of weak tea in my hands. The doctor had declared the immediate danger to the baby had passed, but his warnings about the continued need for rest and calm were absolute. I looked out at the manicured gardens of the townhouse, a small, orderly square of green in the heart of London, and felt a pang of longing for the wild, untamed beauty of Ravenswood.

It was then that Lady Tamsin came to me, her kind face a mixture of relief and a new, more serious gravity.

"He is here, my dear," she said softly, her hands smoothing the covers on the bed I had just vacated. "He has been here every day, waiting in the hall like a lost soul. He has not demanded to see you. He has only... waited." She turned to face me, her gaze direct and full of a fierce, protective love. "He asks for you now. If you are strong enough. But if you are not, Marietta, you have only to say the word, and I will send him away. You need not see him until you are ready."

I looked at my aunt-in-law, at the unwavering loyalty in her eyes, and I felt a surge of profound gratitude. She was offering me a shield, a respite. But I knew I could not hide behind it forever. We could not continue like this, two wounded ghosts haunting separate houses, our marriage a ruin of misunderstanding and unspoken truths. The silence between us was a wound, and if left untended, it would surely fester and poison everything. We had come to the precipice, and there was no turning back. We either had to find a way to cross the chasm between us, or we would both fall.

"Send him in," I whispered, my voice a thin, fragile thing.

I watched the door, my heart a frantic bird against my ribs. I smoothed the lap of my dressing gown, my hands trembling. What would I see? The cold Duke, his face a mask of contemptuous duty? The furious warrior, ready to demand my compliance in his war against my father?

When he entered, my breath caught in my throat. The man who stood before me was a stranger. The formidable, unyielding Duke of Highmoor was gone. In his place was a man who looked utterly, devastatingly broken. His face was pale and drawn, dark shadows etched beneath his eyes. He had not slept. His cravat was slightly askew, a detail so out of character for the impeccably dressed Duke that it was more shocking than any shout. He had not, I suspected, done much of anything but wait, and wrestle with the demons of his own making.

He did not approach me immediately. He stood by the door, his gaze fixed on my face, and in his eyes, I saw none of the anger I had feared. I saw only a raw, unguarded pain, and a shame so profound it was a physical presence in the room. He looked like a man who had seen the full, ugly measure of his own soul and had been found wanting.

"Marietta," he said, his voice a low, rough thing I barely recognized. "Aunt tells me you are... better."

"I am," I said softly.

He walked slowly towards me then, his steps hesitant, as if approaching a frightened animal he did not wish to startle. He did not stop until he reached my chair, and then, with a quiet, weary reverence that shattered the last of my fear, he knelt. He took my hand, his own feeling cool against my skin.

"I have been a monster," he whispered, his gaze fixed on our joined hands. "I have been a blind, arrogant fool. I allowed my own past, my own bitterness, to twist me into a creature I do not recognize. I have endangered you, and our child, with my own unforgivable pride. I know that an apology is a small, inadequate thing in the face of the pain I have caused you. But it is all I have. Forgive me."

His confession, so raw and so complete, left no room for anger. There was only a profound, aching sadness for the both of us, for the terrible, lonely battles we had both been fighting in silence. He had seen his own part in this tragedy, and the weight of his guilt was a visible, crushing thing.

He looked up then, and the raw, naked pain in his eyes was so profound it took my breath away. "I should have seen you. Truly seen you. But I was so consumed by my own ghosts, I could not see yours." He took a deep, shuddering breath, a sound that seemed torn from the very depths of his soul. "I came here today not just to beg your forgiveness, but to... to finally banish the ghosts that have stood between us. You have trusted me with your truth, Marietta. Now, you must allow me to trust you with mine."

28

The Truxth About Violetta

Callum

I knelt before her, the soft, floral scent of her filling my senses, the fragile warmth of her hand in mine a stark contrast to the cold, dead weight in my own soul. I had spent three days in a self-imposed hell, pacing the hallways of this house, waiting, my mind a relentless torture chamber replaying every one of my sins, every cruel word, every blind assumption. The shame was a physical thing, a sickness in my gut.

But in the long, silent hours of my vigil, a new, clearer resolve had taken root. An apology was not enough. To truly earn her forgiveness, to truly have a chance at building something real from the wreckage I had made, I had to do the one thing I had sworn I would never do. I had to show her my own wound. I had to tell her the truth about Violetta.

It was the most terrifying thing I had ever contemplated. For five years, that secret had been my shield, the source of my icy armor. To speak it aloud would be to make myself utterly, completely vulnerable. But as I looked at my wife's pale, gentle face, I knew it was the only way. She had shown me her deepest wound; I owed her nothing less than my own.

"The ghost that has haunted our marriage," I began, my voice a low, strained thing, "the ghost I have allowed to poison my every thought, my every action... it has a name. And her name is Violetta."

I watched her face, saw the flicker of surprise, of a wary, cautious curiosity in her eyes. I took a deep breath and began to tell the story I had not spoken aloud to another living soul.

"I was not always the man you see before you," I said, my gaze dropping to the intricate pattern of the carpet. "Before... I was younger. More arrogant. I believed the world could be bent to my will through logic and control. I married Violetta not for love, but for duty. It was a suitable match. She was beautiful, well-bred, the daughter of an Earl. I believed that would be enough."

The memory was a taste of ash in my mouth. "She was... a creature of light and of laughter. And I, in my ambition and my pride, tried to cage her. I saw her vivacity not as a gift, but as a frivolity, a distraction from the serious business of our lives. She wanted poetry and parties; I wanted order and influence. I was cold to her. Dismissive. I tried to mold her into the perfect, serene Duchess, and in doing so, I slowly, methodically, crushed her spirit."

I paused, the shame of that admission a heavy weight. "She grew unhappy. Distant. I saw her unhappiness not as a symptom of my own failure as a husband, but as a weakness in her character. A flaw. And then... she sought comfort elsewhere."

I finally looked up, meeting Marietta's wide, compassionate gaze. "She took a lover," I said, the words flat and dead. "I discovered it by accident. A letter, left carelessly on her dressing table. It was not a brief, foolish flirtation. It was a long, passionate affair."

A small, sad sound escaped her lips, a breath of pure empathy. "Oh, Callum," she whispered, her fingers tightening on mine. "I am so sorry."

I saw the flicker of genuine pity in her eyes, but I held up a hand, unable to accept a sympathy I did not feel I deserved. "Do not waste your sympathy on me. My own coldness drove her to it. But the betrayal... it was absolute. And it was not the worst of it." My voice dropped, the final, most shameful piece of the confession the hardest to speak. "She was with child," I whispered. "And it was not mine."

Marietta's hand flew to her mouth, a small, shocked gasp escaping her lips.

"She had intended to pass the child off as the Redwyck heir," I said, my voice a raw, bitter thing. "To bring a bastard into the heart of my house. To be deceived is one thing. But to be so close to being tricked into raising another man's bastard as my own, to have my entire lineage, my entire legacy, threatened by a woman's deceit—that was a betrayal of a different order. It was a violation of the soul."

I turned back to face her, my expression grim. "The night I confronted her with the proof... it was the night she died. The whispers you heard were true in one respect: there was a terrible argument. But she did not fall. And she did not jump."

I took a ragged breath, the next words the hardest I had ever had to speak. "She threw herself down those stairs, Marietta. In a fit of guilt and despair and a terror of the ruin she knew was coming, she took her own life. And the life of the child she carried."

The ugly, brutal truth was finally out, hanging in the quiet, sunlit room.

"I did not push her," I said, my voice breaking. "But I might as well have. My coldness, my pride, my final, cutting words... I drove her to it. I have carried that guilt, that failure, every single day for five years. It is the ghost that has lived with me, the poison that has turned my heart to ice. I was so terrified of being made a fool of again, of being betrayed, that when I saw your own secrets, your own sorrow, I could only see it through the lens of my own past. I did not see a woman in pain. I saw another liar, another schemer. And that blindness, that unforgivable, monstrous blindness, is the sin for which I can never forgive myself."

The confession was complete. I had laid the ugliest, most shameful part of my soul bare before her. I waited for her to recoil, to pull her hand from mine, to look at me with the disgust I so richly deserved.

Instead, she moved closer. She used her free hand to gently wipe away a single, hot tear that had traced a path down my own cheek, a tear I had not even been aware I had shed.

"You were not a monster, Callum," she whispered, her voice a balm of pure, unwavering empathy. "You were a man in pain. A man who was betrayed and who did not know how to heal. We have both been prisoners of our pasts. We have both been fighting ghosts."

As I looked at her, at the profound, unconditional forgiveness in her eyes, a wave of emotion so powerful it threatened to undo me completely washed over me. But before I could speak, before I could confess the full, ugly measure of my own unworthiness, she did something that shattered the last of my defenses.

She took my hand, the one that was not holding hers, and gently, deliberately, she drew it to her. My muscles tensed, my entire being bracing for a rejection I knew I deserved. Instead, she guided my large, trembling palm until it rested on the gentle, firm swell of her abdomen.

The warmth, the undeniable curve of her, the sheer, miraculous reality of the life she carried, was a jolt, a current of pure sensation that shot through me. It was the first time I had touched her like this, not as a Duke assessing the security of his heir, but as a man, invited to feel the presence of his own child. In all my obsessive planning and clinical concern, I had never dared this simple, sacred intimacy.

"If you were a monster," she whispered, her gaze holding mine, her voice thick with unshed tears, "he would not be here. This baby would not have survived the storm between us." Her hand came up to rest over mine, pressing it more firmly against her. "You are not a monster, Callum. You are a father."

The word, spoken with such simple, profound certainty, broke me. A choked, ragged sound was torn from my throat. I stared at our joined hands on the swell of her belly, at the tangible proof of our future, and the last of the ice that had encased my heart for five long years simply shattered into dust.

She leaned forward and pressed a soft, gentle kiss to my lips. It was not a kiss of passion. It was a kiss of acceptance. Of understanding. Of a forgiveness I knew I had not earned.

In that moment, in that quiet, sunlit room, the last of the walls between us crumbled to dust. We were no longer the Duke and Duchess, no longer a scandal and a strategy. We were just Callum and Marietta, two scarred and broken souls who had, against all odds, finally, truly, found each other. And for the first time, the future did not feel like a sentence to be endured, but a path we might, finally, be able to walk together.

29

The First Bricks

Marietta

The truth, once spoken, did not magically heal the wounds of the past. It did not erase the scars. But it let in the light. In the quiet, sunlit sanctuary of my aunt-in-law's guest room, Callum and I sat together, not as adversaries, not as strangers, but as two survivors, surveying the wreckage of our own making.

His confession, a story of a pain so profound and a guilt so deep it had shaped the very man he had become, had not horrified me. It had, in a strange and beautiful way, liberated me. It was the key that unlocked the last, most secret chamber of his heart, and in that shared, shadowed space, I found not a monster, but a man as wounded and as haunted as myself.

When the last of our tears had been shed and a fragile, exhausted peace had settled over us, he rose to his feet. I expected him to leave, to retreat to his own wing and his solitude. Instead, he looked down at me, his expression one of a new, profound, and almost fierce tenderness.

"You are not well enough to walk back to your chambers," he stated, his voice a low, gentle rumble that left no room for argument.

Before I could protest, he bent down and, with an ease that belied his own emotional exhaustion, he lifted me into his arms. A small gasp escaped my lips. I was a grown woman, yet he held me as if I weighed nothing, my head finding a natural resting place in the hollow of his shoulder. My arms, as if with a will of their own, wrapped around his neck.

He carried me from Lady Tamsin's sitting room, giving his aunt a single, grateful nod as we passed. He moved through the long, silent corridors of the house, his steps steady and sure. This was not the frantic, panicked pursuit of a few days ago. This was a slow, deliberate act of care, of protection. I could feel the steady, reassuring beat of his heart against my cheek, feel the strength in the arms that held me.

He did not take me to my own cold, lonely chambers. He took me to his. He carried me into his rooms, a space I had only ever seen in a storm of anger and passion, and gently laid me down on his bed. He pulled the heavy covers over me and then sat on the edge of the mattress, his hand finding mine in the dim light.

"Rest now, Marietta," he whispered. "We will speak more later. For now, just... rest. I will not leave you."

And in that quiet, simple promise, in that act of profound, unexpected tenderness, the first, tentative bricks of a real marriage began to be laid.

I must have drifted into a deep, exhausted sleep, a sleep punctuated by strange, hazy dreams. Sometime in the deep, silent hours of the night, I surfaced, not to full wakefulness, but to a state of soft, blurry awareness. I was aware of a weight, a gentle, warm pressure on my abdomen, and the sound of a low, rumbling voice, a voice so full of a raw, broken sorrow it seemed to be a part of the darkness itself.

"*Forgive me, little one,*" the voice whispered, a sound so close it seemed to be spoken directly against my skin. "*Forgive your father for being such a blind, cruel fool. For hurting your mother... for not knowing...*"

The words were a gentle, aching caress, a balm on a wound I did not know I had. It was a dream, I thought, a beautiful, impossible dream born of my own desperate longing. And I sank back into the welcoming darkness, the memory of his whispered apology a sweet, sad lullaby.

When I next opened my eyes, the heavy damask curtains were drawn against the morning sun, casting the room in a soft, dim twilight. For a moment,

I was disoriented, the unfamiliar ceiling and the faint, masculine scent of sandalwood and old books reminding me that I was not in my own chambers. I was in his.

I turned my head slowly on the pillow. He was still there. Callum had not left me. He had fallen asleep in the large armchair he had pulled up to the bedside, his body slumped in a posture of pure, unadulterated exhaustion. His head was tipped back against the rich burgundy leather, his long legs stretched out before him.

For the first time since I had met him, I saw my husband not as the formidable Duke, but simply as a man, stripped of all his icy armor. And he was a complete mess. The man who was always so impeccably, so flawlessly put together, looked utterly undone. A dark shadow of stubble covered his strong jaw, a testament to at least a day and a night without seeing his valet. His dark hair, usually cut short and severe, was longer now, softened by sleep, a stray lock falling across his forehead in a way that was surprisingly boyish. The fine lawn of his shirt was rumpled, his cravat long since discarded.

He looked weary, vulnerable, and more handsome than I had ever allowed myself to admit. The cold, hard mask he presented to the world was gone, and in its place was a man who had clearly been tormented by worry. My worry. And then I saw it. Faint, almost invisible in the dim light, but undeniably there: the dried, salty track of a single tear on his cheek, stark against the dark stubble. My dream had not been a dream at all.

Moved by an impulse so tender it felt like an ache in my chest, I slowly, carefully, pushed myself up. The bed was large, and I was able to slip out from under the covers without disturbing him. I padded silently across the thick carpet until I stood beside his chair. I knelt on the floor, my own movements slow and careful, mindful of the precious weight I carried. I was now close enough to see the faint, dark lashes that rested against his pale skin, the weary lines etched around his eyes.

My hand lifted, as if with a will of its own. I hesitated for a single, heart-stopping second, and then I reached out and laid my palm gently against the rough warmth of his cheek.

The small, simple touch was enough. His dark lashes fluttered open. His grey eyes, hazy and unfocused with sleep, found my face. For a moment, there was only a quiet, sleepy confusion. Then, as recognition dawned, a look of immediate, sharp concern replaced the softness.

"Marietta?" he murmured, his voice a low, rough rasp from sleep. "Are you alright? Do you require something?"

A slow, genuine smile, the first truly effortless smile I had given him, touched my lips. I shook my head, my hand still resting on his cheek. "No," I whispered. "I require nothing. It is you... you are a mess, Your Grace."

A ghost of a smile, a faint, weary curve of his own mouth, answered mine. He turned his head slightly, pressing his cheek more firmly into my palm. He captured my hand with his own, bringing it to his lips and pressing a soft, warm kiss into the center of my palm. The gesture was so full of a quiet, unassuming tenderness it stole the very breath from my lungs.

"I confess I have not had much time for my valet," he said, his voice still rough. "The work has been... demanding."

I knew it was a lie. A kind, noble lie to spare me from the truth. The work that had exhausted him, the worry that had etched those lines on his face, was me. It was the frantic, desperate fear he had felt when he thought he might lose me, might lose our child. And in that lie, in that simple, protective gesture, I felt a wave of love for him so powerful it was almost painful.

I leaned forward, my body resting against the arm of his chair, my head finding a natural place in the curve of his shoulder. He did not stiffen. He did not pull away. His arm came around me, holding me close, his other hand still holding mine.

My own free hand came to rest on the gentle, firm swell of my abdomen. At nearly eighteen weeks, there was no denying the new life within. My belly was a soft, rounded curve, a tangible, miraculous promise.

"He is moving," I whispered into the quiet of the room.

I felt him tense slightly, a new, more profound stillness coming over him.

I took his hand, the one that was holding mine, and gently, deliberately, I drew it to me. I guided his large, warm palm until it rested on the curve of my belly, directly over the place where our son was stirring.

"I know you have been afraid," I said softly, my voice a little thick. "But he is strong. And he deserves to feel his father's touch. At least once."

I felt his hand tremble beneath mine. It was not a small tremor; it was a violent, shuddering quake, the tremor of a man's entire world shifting on its foundations. I held it there, my own hand a steady anchor over his. A moment passed, and then another, and he remained utterly, completely still.

Finally, I lifted my gaze to his face. And what I saw broke my heart.

My husband, the formidable Duke of Ice, the man of iron and control, was weeping. Tears were streaming silently, unashamedly, down his face, carving shining paths through the dark stubble on his cheeks.

"Callum?" I whispered, my own eyes filling with tears in response.

"I never..." he began, his voice a raw, broken thing, thick with an emotion so profound he could barely speak. "I never thought... I was afraid to ask. Afraid to hope." He looked down at his own hand on my stomach as if it were a foreign object, a thing of wonder and of terror. "He is truly there."

"Yes," I whispered.

"I want this," he said, his voice cracking, his gaze finally lifting to meet mine, his eyes a turbulent storm of a pain and a joy so immense it was humbling. "Marietta, I want to be a father more than I have ever wanted anything in my entire life. I have never, not for a moment, been unwilling to touch my own child."

I reached up with my free hand and gently, reverently, wiped a tear from his cheek with my thumb. His skin was rough, his tears were hot. He was real. This was real.

"I know," I whispered. I leaned in, my lips hovering just inches from his. "You are not just going to be a father, Callum."

His breath hitched, his tear-filled eyes wide with a desperate, questioning hope.

"You already are one," I breathed, and then I closed the final distance between us and kissed him, a kiss not of passion, but of promise, a seal on a truth that had, against all odds, finally brought us home.

30

A Husband's Care

Callum

The morning sun, a pale but determined thing, streamed through the tall windows of my dressing room, illuminating the small, domestic scene that had, improbably, become the new center of my world. The air was warm, thick with the scent of shaving soap and the faint, floral perfume that clung to my wife like a second skin.

She stood before me, her brow furrowed in a mask of intense concentration, a straight razor held with a surprising, steady confidence in her hand. Her other hand rested gently on my jaw, tilting my head to just the right angle. I sat in the chair, a towel draped around my shoulders, and submitted to her care with a sense of quiet wonder that was still, after all this time, a new and precious thing.

My valet, a man who had served me with stoic perfection for over a decade, had nearly fainted from shock the first time Marietta had dismissed him, insisting that tending to her husband's morning toilette was a wife's privilege. I had not argued. To feel her hands on my skin, to exist in this quiet, shared intimacy, had become a necessary part of my day, a simple, profound ritual that grounded me in this new, unbelievable reality of a shared life.

"Hold still," she murmured, her voice a soft, chiding thing. "Or the Duke of Highmoor shall be forced to attend Parliament with a plaster on his chin."

"A fate worse than death, I am certain," I replied, my voice a low rumble. I watched her, the way a stray lock of dark hair had escaped her pins to curl against her cheek, the focused, determined press of her lips. A wave of love, so fierce and so profound it was a physical ache in my chest, washed over me.

A memory, sharp and unwelcome, surfaced of Violetta, who would have considered such a domestic task a tedious bore, something to be left to the servants. But the fault was not entirely hers, I admitted with a familiar, bitter pang of guilt. I had been a different man then, a cold, ambitious Duke who would never have permitted such a casual, profound intimacy. I had never given her the chance to be a wife in this way. With Marietta, I was determined not to make the same mistake. This simple act was a redemption, a quiet vow to be the man she deserved.

My thoughts were drawn back to the present as she finished the final, smooth stroke of the razor and began to wipe the last of the soap from my skin with a warm, damp cloth. Her touch was impossibly gentle, a soft caress that grounded me in the here and now. She surveyed her work, a small, satisfied smile playing on her lips.

"There," she declared. "Respectable once more."

Her task was done, but she did not move away. Instead, she picked up a pair of shears from the dressing table. "Now," she said, her eyes sparkling with a new, more mischievous light, "for that mess you call your hair. It has grown quite unruly, Your Grace."

That was a bridge too far. Before she could snip a single, ill-advised lock, my hand shot out and captured her wrist. With a gentle but firm tug, I pulled her off balance and onto my lap. She landed with a soft, surprised gasp, the shears clattering harmlessly to the floor.

"Callum!" she cried, a lovely flush rising on her cheeks.

"I am a man of many newfound faiths, my love," I said, my voice a low, teasing rumble against her ear as my arms wrapped around her, holding her securely against my chest. "But my faith in your skills as a barber is, I confess, not yet fully formed."

"Are you saying you do not trust me?" she asked, a mock-pout on her lips.

"I trust you with my life," I murmured, my lips finding the sensitive skin of her neck. "But my ducal reputation is another matter entirely. I must remain at least passably handsome, so that my wife may continue to show me off with pride."

"My husband is far too handsome for his own good," she whispered back, her own arms now circling my neck, her body melting against mine. "It is a trial I must bear with great fortitude."

A low, warm laugh rumbled in my chest. "Do not pretend you are not as impatient as I am, my love."

I did not wait for her reply. I tightened my hold on her, and she shifted on my lap, her body molding perfectly to mine. I tilted my head and kissed her. It was not the desperate, frantic kiss of our past conflicts, nor the careful, questioning kisses of our early reconciliation. This was something else entirely. It was a kiss of deep, sweet, and lingering possession, a kiss that tasted of soap and of a quiet, domestic happiness I had never believed I would know.

Her lips were soft, parting for me with a gentle, trusting sigh. I kissed her slowly, reverently, my tongue tracing the seam of her mouth before deepening the kiss. One of my hands moved from her waist to her face, my thumb stroking the soft curve of her cheek, while my other hand remained spread protectively over the firm, proud swell of her abdomen. To kiss her like this, while holding both her and our child, was an act of such profound, humbling intimacy that it made my heart ache. It was a kiss that sealed not just our present peace, but our future promise.

As she sat on my lap, my hands moved of their own accord, a natural, instinctual gesture, to rest on the firm, proud swell of her abdomen. My palms spread over the curve, a silent, protective, and deeply possessive gesture. It was a part of me now, this constant, unconscious connection to her, and to the child who grew within her. It was the most natural, most right thing in the world. The future was here, warm and real, a living, breathing thing in my arms.

31

The Absolute Priority

When I was finally strong enough to leave my room, she summoned us not to the formal drawing room, but to her own private sitting room, a cozy, comfortable space filled with chintz furniture, overflowing bookshelves, and the scent of lemon verbena. A fire crackled in the hearth, a cheerful, steady presence against the lingering chill of the autumn afternoon. She served us tea herself, her movements calm and deliberate, creating an atmosphere not of confrontation, but of quiet, familial council.

Isabelle, I knew, was out for a long walk in the park with her governess. It was a deliberate, considerate act on Lady Tamsin's part, a way to give us the space to speak of her without the painful, beautiful presence of the child herself.

We sat, the three of us, in a small triangle around the hearth. Callum was beside me on the settee, his presence a warm, solid, and reassuring weight. His hand rested on mine, his thumb stroking the back of my hand in a slow, steady rhythm, a silent, constant affirmation of his support, of his presence.

"We have a great deal to discuss," Lady Tamsin began, her voice gentle but firm, leaving no room for evasion. She looked at me, her eyes full of a new, profound, and aching sympathy. "My dear child, my heart breaks for the pain you have endured. And for my own part in it, however unwitting, I am so deeply sorry."

"You have nothing to be sorry for, Aunt," I whispered, my voice thick with emotion. "You gave my daughter a home. You gave her your love. You saved her. There is no apology necessary for an act of such profound kindness."

She gave me a small, watery smile. "Nevertheless. The past is the past. We cannot change it. We can only decide what we are to do with the present. And our present, my dears, is a very... complicated thing." She turned her gaze to her nephew, her expression one of both love and a new, more serious gravity. "Callum, I know your first instinct, now that you know the truth, will be to seek justice. To confront the Viscount, to unleash the full force of your ducal power upon him and his family for the monstrous thing they have done."

I felt Callum's hand tighten on mine, a confirmation of her words. I looked at his face, at the hard, unyielding set of his jaw, and I saw the warrior, the Duke, the man who was ready to go to war for me.

"He is right to do so," he said, his voice a low, dangerous rumble. "What they did was not just a cruelty; it was a crime. They stole your child, Marietta. They condemned you to years of torment. They will not go unpunished."

"And what would that punishment look like?" Lady Tamsin asked quietly, her voice a calm, steady anchor in the storm of his anger. "A public scandal? A lawsuit? A duel, perhaps? And what would be the outcome of such a war, Callum? The world would learn that your wife, the Duchess of Highmoor, bore an illegitimate child. And Isabelle, our sweet, innocent Isabelle, would be branded a bastard in the eyes of the law and of society. Her name, her future, her very identity, would be destroyed. Is that a justice you are willing to pursue?"

Her words, so logical and so brutal, struck the air from the room. Callum's anger, which had been a righteous, blazing fire, seemed to bank, replaced by a new, more complex and frustrating reality. He was a man accustomed to winning, to vanquishing his enemies. But this was a battle where victory itself would mean a catastrophic loss.

"There must be a way," he insisted, but his voice had lost its hard edge, replaced by a weary frustration. "To make him pay, without..."

"Without destroying the very people you seek to protect?" his aunt finished gently. "Perhaps, in time. But for now, our first and only priority must be the children." She turned her gaze back to me, and it was full of a soft, maternal warmth. "Both of them."

My hand instinctively went to my own abdomen, a gesture of unconscious, protective love. The other child. The secret I had only just confessed to Callum, the fragile, precious life that was the reason for this entire, terrifying crisis.

"I want to tell her," I said, the words a quiet, desperate plea that came straight from the heart of my own maternal agony. "I want to tell Isabelle the truth. I cannot bear the thought of living another day with this lie between us. She is my daughter. She has a right to know who her mother is."

I looked from my aunt's kind face to my husband's, searching for their understanding, for their support.

It was Callum who spoke first, his voice a low, gentle thing, but his words were a denial nonetheless. "She is three years old, Marietta," he said softly. "How could we possibly explain this to her? What would we say? That the woman she knows as her loving 'Mama Tamsin' is not her mother? That her 'Aunt Marietta' is a stranger who gave her away? The truth, at her age, would not be a comfort. It would be a confusion, a terror. It would shatter her entire world."

"But to continue the lie feels so… wrong," I whispered, the tears I had thought long spent once again burning behind my eyes. "Every time she calls me 'Aunt', it is a knife in my heart. I want to be her mother. Not in secret. Not from a distance."

"And you will be," Lady Tamsin said, her voice firm but kind. "In time. But we must be patient. We must be clever. For her sake." She leaned forward, her expression one of the utmost seriousness. "And for the sake of the child you are now carrying."

The words hung in the air, a stark and undeniable truth.

"Marietta," she said, her voice softening. "You are in a delicate, fragile state. The doctor was most clear. Your health, and the health of this baby, must be our absolute priority. To engage in a battle with your father now, to unravel the complex legal and social tangle of Isabelle's parentage, to subject yourself to that kind of emotional turmoil… it is a risk we simply cannot afford to take. This new baby, this Redwyck heir, deserves its chance at life. A chance that must not be threatened by the scandals of the past."

Her logic was a cold, inescapable cage. Every word she spoke was true, and every truth tightened the bonds around me, forcing me to choose between two loves, two children. To fight for Isabelle now would be to risk the child I carried. My own selfish, desperate need to be known as a mother had to be secondary to the well-being of them both.

I looked at Callum, my last, desperate hope. But I saw in his eyes a reflection of his aunt's own grim, protective resolve. He, who had been so terrified of losing this new heir, would not countenance any action, however just, that might put it at risk.

My shoulders slumped in defeat. The fire of my maternal desperation sputtered and died, leaving only the cold ash of resignation. They were right. They were brutally, horribly right. Silence, for now, was the only protection I could offer to everyone I loved.

"Very well," I whispered, the words a taste of surrender in my mouth. "We will wait. We will keep the secret. For the children."

A fragile, unspoken agreement was made in that quiet, sunlit room. We would not confront my father. We would not reveal the truth. We would simply... be. A strange, secret, and complicated family. Callum would continue to be Isabelle's 'cousin'. I would continue to be her 'aunt'. And Lady Tamsin would continue to be her mother, in all the ways that truly mattered.

It was not the reunion I had dreamed of. It was not the justice I had craved. It was a compromise, a painful, necessary sacrifice. It was the first, difficult brick in a long and uncertain road to healing. But as Callum's hand tightened on mine, a silent, steady promise of a shared burden, I knew, for the first time, that it was a road I would not have to walk alone.

32

A Promise to Keep

Marietta

The two weeks that Lady Tamsin and Isabelle remained in London passed in a blur of quiet, domestic peace that was both a profound blessing and an exquisite form of torture. The house, once a cold and silent mausoleum, was filled with the sound of a child's laughter, a constant, beautiful melody that soothed the raw edges of my soul. I soaked in every moment, hoarding them like a miser hoarding gold. There was the afternoon Isabelle, with a face of the utmost seriousness, insisted on serving me a pretend tea of water and a single, crumbled biscuit. There was the morning she fell asleep with her head in my lap as I read to her, her small body a warm, trusting weight, her soft breath puffing against my arm. For these fleeting, stolen moments, I was not a Duchess, not a wife, not a secret. I was simply... a mother.

But like all beautiful dreams, it had to end.

The day of their departure arrived with a cool, grey morning that perfectly matched the sorrow in my heart. The traveling carriage was brought to the front of the house, its dark lacquered panels gleaming like the shell of a funeral beetle. The trunks were carried down, each thud on the marble floor a countdown to the moment I would have to say goodbye again. This was the second severing. The first had been an act of brutal, violent theft by my father. This, somehow, felt worse. This was a slow, deliberate amputation, an act I had to participate in with a serene smile on my face.

We gathered in the grand hall for the final farewells. Lady Tamsin, dressed for the journey in a pelisse of deep blue velvet, embraced me warmly.

"You must take care of yourself, my dear," she whispered, her kind eyes full of a knowing, gentle affection. "And of my future grand-nephew or niece. We shall expect a letter the very moment there is news."

"Of course," I murmured, my throat tight, the words a painful lump I could barely force past.

Then, Isabelle was there. She stood before me, a small, perfect figure in her own tiny traveling cloak, her expression a mask of quiet sorrow. My heart broke. It simply cracked in two in my chest. This was it. The moment I had been dreading, the moment my soul had been screaming against for days.

I knelt down, so that we were at eye level. I did not care who was watching. The servants, the footmen, my husband—they all faded into an indistinct, grey blur. There was only this child, my child, and the few precious seconds I had left.

"I have to go away for a little while, Aunt Marietta," she whispered, her small lower lip trembling.

The words were a knife in my heart. She was comforting *me*. A fresh wave of guilt, so profound it was sickening, washed over me. I pulled her into a fierce, desperate embrace, my arms wrapping around her as if I could somehow absorb her into myself, keep her with me through sheer force of will. I buried my face in the soft, fragrant cloud of her dark curls. She smelled of sweet soap and sunshine, a scent I knew would haunt my dreams for the rest of my days. I held her tight, trying to memorize the feel of her small, warm body against mine, the impossible, miraculous weight of her in my arms. This is what it feels like to hold your own heart. And I am about to let it go.

"I know, my darling," I whispered back, my voice thick with unshed tears. "But I will come and visit you at Ravenswood. Very soon. I promise."

The promise was a vow, a sacred oath I made not just to her, but to myself. I would not lose her again.

I pulled back, forcing a smile onto my lips, a watery, wavering thing. It was then that her gaze dropped to my stomach, which was now a pronounced, gentle curve beneath my morning gown. My other child. The one I would be allowed to keep. The one whose existence made this separation from my firstborn a unique and complicated agony. My hand instinctively came up to rest on the swell, a gesture of protection and of a deep, abiding guilt.

Isabelle's small hand, hesitant at first, reached out and rested on my belly, just below my own. The innocent, trusting touch was a jolt, a current of pure, agonizing joy that shot through me. It was the touch of a sister. My two children, who did not know each other, were connected for one, brief, miraculous moment.

"Mama Tamsin says you have a baby sister for me in there," she said, her green eyes, *my* green eyes, wide with a solemn, childish wonder. "You must bring her with you when you come to visit. So I can teach her how to play."

The simple, beautiful request was my undoing. To hear her speak of her future sibling, a sister she did not know was truly her own, with such sweet, uncomplicated acceptance... it was a glimpse of the family we could be, the family we should have been. A tear I could no longer hold back spilled over and traced a hot path down my cheek. Before I could find the words to answer, a warm, steady presence knelt beside us.

It was Callum. He placed a gentle hand on Isabelle's head, his fingers stroking her dark curls.

"She will," he said, his voice a low, soft thing, full of a warmth that enveloped us both. "Your Aunt Marietta and I will bring your new cousin to visit as soon as they are old enough to travel. And I am quite certain," he added, his grey eyes meeting mine over the top of our daughter's head, a silent, steady promise in their depths, "that they will be very eager to learn."

He stood, gently helping me to my feet. The moment was over. It was time to go. I gave Isabelle one last, lingering look, searing the image of her small, sad face into my memory. And then I turned and walked to the carriage, my heart a cold, heavy stone in my chest, leaving a piece of my soul behind me on the cold marble floor of the grand hall.

33

A Future in Hand

Callum

The silence in my bedchamber was of a quality I had never known. It was not the hostile void of our early days, nor the charged, aching silence of our misunderstandings. It was a soft, peaceful quiet, a space for healing, filled not with unspoken accusations, but with a profound, unspoken understanding.

Marietta sat on my lap, her body a warm, trusting weight against mine. She was curled against my chest, her head resting in the hollow of my shoulder, a book of poetry lying open but forgotten beside us. My arm was around her, my hand resting gently on the pronounced, perfect curve of her abdomen. They were simple gestures, small intimacies that would be commonplace for any other married couple. For us, they were a revolution. They were the first, tentative words in a new language we were only just beginning to learn.

"Are you comfortable?" I murmured, my voice a low rumble against her hair.

She shifted slightly, tilting her head back to look up at me with a soft, sleepy smile. "I cannot imagine being more so," she whispered, her voice full of a genuine, quiet contentment. She paused, a gentle tease entering her eyes. "Though I confess, I never pictured you as a man who would tolerate having his circulation cut off for the sake of sentimental poetry."

A genuine, easy laugh escaped me, a sound that was still unfamiliar in these grand, silent rooms. "The poetry was merely an excuse. It is the company I find I cannot do without."

I looked down at her, at the dark, silken crown of her head, at the sweep of her lashes against her pale cheek. The storm within her had not vanished, I knew, but it had finally found a calm harbor. And I, against all odds, was that harbor. The realization was a humbling, terrifying, and profoundly sacred thing.

The secrets that had been a chasm between us were now a bridge. Her truth, a story of a cruelty so profound it still made my blood run cold with a righteous fury, had not repulsed me. It had, in its own strange way, healed me. In the depths of her pain, I had been forced to confront the shallowness of my own. My wounds, which I had nursed for five years, had been wounds of pride, of a betrayed honor. Hers were the wounds of a mother, a primal, fundamental grief that made my own suffering seem a small and selfish thing.

She had trusted me. Even after my cruelty, my suspicion, my monstrous misjudgment, she had looked at me and seen a man worthy of her truth. And in that gift of trust, she had given me a path back to myself, back to the man I had been before Violetta's betrayal had turned my heart to stone. She had shown me that vulnerability was not a weakness, but a strength.

My hand moved, my thumb stroking a slow, gentle circle on the taut silk of her gown, right over the swell of our child. "I find myself thinking of him constantly," I confessed, the words a quiet admission in the firelit room. "Wondering if he will have your eyes."

"And your stubbornness, I am quite certain," she whispered, a gentle tease in her voice. "He will be a formidable debater in the nursery, mark my words."

"God help me," I chuckled. "I shall teach him to ride before he can properly walk. He will have the best seat in all of England."

Marietta laughed softly, a sound that was pure music. She tilted her head, her green eyes sparkling with mischief. "I fear you will be disappointed, Your Grace. He will much prefer reading poetry in the parlor with his mother. He is destined to be utterly devoted to me."

A low, warm laugh rumbled in my chest. "Is he now?" I murmured, leaning in to press a kiss to her temple. "Then we shall simply have to have another. A daughter for you, and the heir for me. A perfectly fair division, I think."

"Only two?" she teased, her eyes sparkling as she tilted her head back to look at me. "That hardly seems a fair number for a Duke of your stature. Should we not aim for five?"

I considered this with mock seriousness. "Five would be a respectable start," I conceded. "Though if they all have your spirit, Duchess, I fear our governess will demand a salary commensurate with that of a field marshal."

"And if they all have your stubbornness, they will not listen to a word she says anyway," she retorted softly.

I laughed again, a sound of pure, uncomplicated joy. I pulled her closer, my lips finding her temple. "Then we must have as many as possible," I murmured against her skin. "I find I am exceedingly greedy for more children who resemble their mother."

Her arms tightened around my neck, and she pressed a soft kiss to my jaw. "And I for more who resemble their father."

I looked into her eyes, my own heart aching with a love so profound it was a physical thing. "In that case, my love," I said, my voice a low, suggestive rumble, "it seems we have a great deal of work ahead of us. At least a decade's worth, I should think."

This small, private room had become our entire world, a sanctuary from the ghosts that haunted the rest of the house. A new, unfamiliar emotion, as bright and as fragile as the morning sun, was beginning to dawn in my soul. It was not the possessive, desperate desire I had felt for her before. It was something quieter, deeper, and infinitely more powerful. A fierce, protective tenderness. A quiet, profound respect. A slow, burgeoning, and terrifying love.

"He is quiet this evening," I murmured.

She shifted slightly again, her hand coming up to cover mine where it rested on her belly. "He has been listening to you," she whispered, her smile soft. "He is as captivated by your stories of parliamentary debate as I am."

I feigned a wounded look. "Are you implying my political discourse is a

181

cure for insomnia, Duchess?"

"I am implying," she said, her eyes sparkling, "that he finds his father's voice as soothing as I do."

I lowered my head and kissed her then, a soft, lingering kiss that tasted of tea and of hope.

The weight of our shared future was a heavy, momentous thing. There were still battles to be fought. Her father, the Viscount, would still have to be dealt with, though now with a cold, strategic precision rather than a hot, ducal rage. And there was the question of Isabelle, a question so complex and so delicate it would require all the patience and wisdom we possessed.

But for the first time, these challenges did not feel like solitary burdens. They were ours to face, together. As I held this strange, strong, and beautiful woman who was my wife, I felt not the weight of a duty, but the profound, humbling grace of a second chance. And beneath my hand, beneath hers, I felt a sudden, strong flutter—a kick.

My breath hitched. My entire being went still, focused on that single point of contact, a secret message from a world away.

Marietta laughed softly, a beautiful, musical sound. "It seems he disagrees with your latest policy, Your Grace."

I looked from our joined hands on her belly to her radiant face, my own eyes wide with a wonder so profound it felt like a form of prayer. It was real. This was all real. My wife. Our son. Our future. It was all here, a tangible, living thing in my arms, under my hand.

A sudden, fierce memory of her confession, of the horrors she had endured giving birth to Isabelle, flashed through my mind. The leather strap, the forbidden screams, the cold cruelty of her father. A protective rage, so potent it was a physical force, rose in me.

I pulled her closer, my lips finding her temple. "Marietta," I murmured, my voice thick with an emotion I could not name. "When the time comes... for him... I want you to know something."

She tilted her head back, her green eyes searching mine, wide and questioning.

"There will be no leather strap," I said, my voice a low, fierce vow. "There will be no silence. You may scream the rafters down. You may curse my name. You may break every bone in my hand if you wish."

A watery, teasing light entered her eyes, a flicker of the playful woman she was becoming with me. "And may I pull your hair?" she whispered.

A low chuckle rumbled in my chest. "You may scalp me, my love, if it gives you a moment's relief." My expression grew serious again as I leaned my forehead against hers, my gaze intense and absolute. "This time, you will not be alone. I will be with you. And you will be safe. I swear it."

Tears welled in her eyes, but a small, trembling smile touched her lips. "And... and if he is a she? If it is a daughter? You would not be... disappointed?"

The question, so full of a past fear of failing to meet a man's expectations, made my heart ache. "Disappointed?" I murmured, my hand coming up to gently cup her jaw. "Marietta, to have another girl in this house with the spirit and the light of Isabelle would be the greatest blessing I could imagine. A son, a daughter... it does not matter. As long as they are ours, and they are healthy."

The tears finally spilled over then, but they were not tears of sorrow or fear. They were tears of a profound, healing gratitude. She buried her face in my shoulder, her body shaking with a quiet sob.

"I will scream," she whispered, her voice muffled against my coat. "When the pain comes, this time, I will scream so loud."

I held her tighter, pressing a kiss to the crown of her head. "Then you will scream," I said, my voice a firm, unwavering promise. "You may scream so loud the whole of London hears you and believes the sky is falling. I do not care if you deafen every man in this house. All that matters, the only thing that matters, is that you are safe."

The tears that welled in her eyes this time were not of sorrow or fear. They were tears of a profound, healing gratitude. And in that moment, in the quiet intimacy of our chamber, the last of the ice around my heart simply melted away.

34

The Dearest Man

Marietta

Hope, I discovered, was a quiet and tentative thing. It did not arrive with a clap of thunder or a blaze of light. It seeped into the cracked and barren landscape of my heart slowly, like a gentle spring rain, coaxing new, fragile green shoots from the scorched earth.

The weeks following were the most peaceful of my life. The grand, imposing fortress of Redwyck House, which had once been my gilded prison, began, improbably, to feel like a home. The oppressive silence was gone, replaced by the soft, easy quiet of a shared life. It was a quiet filled with the rustle of a newspaper in the morning room, the low murmur of Callum's voice from his study, the distant, cheerful sound of a new nursery being prepared.

The change in Callum was a daily miracle. The formidable, icy Duke had retreated, and in his place was the man I had glimpsed at the country inn, the man who had knelt at my feet in his aunt's sitting room. He was a man of quiet, profound kindness, his every action a silent, steady apology for the pain he had caused me.

He was attentive to my health with a new, gentle concern that was worlds away from his previous clinical obsession. The change began the week Dr. Arbuthnot came for his now-regular visit. I was nearly five months along, my belly a firm, proud curve beneath my morning gown, a constant, miraculous presence. Callum insisted on being there, as always, but his demeanor was different. He was not the cold, watchful sentinel of before, but a nervous, expectant father.

He stood by the window while the doctor performed his gentle examination, his hands clasped so tightly behind his back that his knuckles were white. Dr. Arbuthnot, after listening for the heartbeat with his conical tube, finally straightened up, his kind face wreathed in a genuine smile.

"His Grace is a strong one, Your Grace," the doctor announced cheerfully. "A heartbeat as steady and as robust as a drum major's. You are both in excellent health. Continue with your rest and your gentle walks, and I see no reason why we should not expect a fine, healthy Redwyck heir come the spring."

The relief that washed over Callum's face was a profound, unguarded thing. The rigid tension left his shoulders, and he gave the doctor a nod of such profound gratitude it was more eloquent than any words. After the doctor left, Callum did not retreat to his study. He came to me, his hand reaching out, not with the clinical assessment of before, but with a new, reverent wonder, and rested it on the swell of my stomach. He no longer saw me as a fragile vessel for his heir; he saw *me*, and the child we had created together.

From that day on, his care transformed. He would still insist I rest on the chaise longue in the afternoon, but he would not leave me to my solitude. He would pull up a chair and read to me, his voice a low, soothing rumble, the words of a political treatise or a dry historical text made strangely intimate by the simple act of him sharing them with me.

One afternoon, he found me in the sunroom, staring out at the gardens, my hand resting on the gentle, growing swell of my abdomen. He came to stand behind me, and for a long moment, we simply stood in a shared, peaceful silence, watching the autumn leaves drift from the trees. Then, his hands came to rest on my shoulders, his touch a warm, comforting weight. He leaned down, his cheek brushing against my hair, and his own hand came to join mine on my stomach.

He leaned down, his cheek brushing against my hair, and his own hand came to join mine on my stomach.

"Has he been moving today?" he whispered, his voice a raw, husky thing against my ear.

"He has been quiet for the last hour," I whispered back, my heart so full I felt it might burst. "I think he is sleeping."

A low chuckle rumbled in his chest, a warm vibration against my back. "A tendency for sleeping in," he murmured, his voice laced with amusement. "I wonder from which side of the family he inherits that particular trait."

"Certainly not from his mother," I teased softly. "I have been awake since dawn listening to you snore."

He was about to offer a retort when a sudden, strong flutter erupted beneath our hands—a definitive, indignant kick. Callum's breath hitched, his entire body going still.

I laughed, a soft, joyful sound. "It seems he heard you. He is a sensitive soul, it appears. He does not appreciate being called a sluggard."

Callum let out a slow breath, a sound of pure, unadulterated wonder. "Already so easily offended," he said, his voice thick with an emotion I could not name. "He will be a true Redwyck, then."

We stood there, a husband and a wife, a father and a mother, his hand covering mine, both of us focused on the tiny, secret life that bound us together. In that moment, the ghosts of the past, of Violetta, of Julian, of my father's cruelty, seemed to recede, their power diminished by the simple, profound reality of this new, shared hope.

The physical intimacy between us returned, not with the desperate, angry fire of before, but with a new, tender, and almost reverent quality. Our bedchamber was no longer a cold and lonely space, but a sanctuary. He would come to me at night, his movements slow, his gaze a soft, searching thing. Our lovemaking was a quiet, unhurried exploration, a rediscovery of each other's bodies on a new foundation of profound trust and love.

He would undress me slowly, his hands tracing the faint, silvery lines on my stomach, not with a questioning shock, but with a gentle, aching sadness for the pain they represented. He would kiss those scars, an act of such profound, healing tenderness that tears would stream down my face, tears not of sorrow, but of a gratitude so immense it was overwhelming.

In his arms, I felt not like Lady Ruin, not like a disgraced and fallen woman, but like someone cherished, someone beautiful, someone whole. He was not just taking his pleasure; he was worshipping me, healing me with the slow, patient reverence of his touch. And I, in turn, gave myself to him completely, my body and my heart finally, irrevocably, united in its surrender.

We were a real couple now, sharing the small, quiet moments that are the true architecture of a marriage. We would talk for hours in the firelit darkness of our room, our voices low, sharing stories, hopes, and fears. He spoke more of his past, of the lonely, duty-bound boy he had been, and I, in turn, found the courage to speak of mine, not of the great, dramatic tragedy, but of the small, simple girl I had been before it all.

The subject of Isabelle was a constant, gentle presence between us. We spoke of her often, our voices a mixture of love and a shared, aching sorrow for the lie we were forced to live.

"My aunt writes that she asks for you every day," he said one evening, his hand stroking my hair as I lay with my head on his chest.

"And I for her," I whispered, a familiar pang in my heart.

"We will find a way, Marietta," he said, his voice a firm, steady promise. "When the time is right, when you and the baby are strong, we will face your father. We will find a way to bring her into our lives, to have her know her true place with us. I will not let you be separated from her forever. You have my word."

His promise was a balm on my soul, a steady anchor in the turbulent sea of my own uncertainty. The path ahead was not clear. It was fraught with danger and with the potential for a catastrophic scandal. But I knew, with a certainty that settled deep in my bones, that I would not have to face it alone. I had a partner. An ally. A husband.

The fragile hope that had been born in the wreckage of our confessions was no longer so fragile. It was growing, day by day, into a strong and steady flame, a beacon of light in the long, dark night of my past. We were two scarred and broken people, yes, but we were rebuilding, together, laying the first, tentative bricks of a future that might, just might, be more beautiful than anything either of us had ever dared to imagine.

35

A Future in Sight

Callum

The journey back to London was a quiet affair, but the silence was of a quality I had never known. It was not the hostile void of our early days, nor the charged, aching silence of our misunderstandings. It was a soft, peaceful quiet, a space for healing, filled not with unspoken accusations, but with a profound, unspoken understanding.

We were returning from a two-day visit to my estate in Kent, a necessary trip to inspect the spring planting. It was the first time we had traveled alone together since the disastrous journey that had ended in my study with her confession. This journey was a different world entirely.

The late afternoon sunlight, a pale, golden thing, slanted through the carriage window, illuminating the woman beside me. Marietta was asleep, her head resting on my shoulder, one hand tucked trustingly into the crook of my arm. The faint, bruised shadows that had once been a permanent fixture beneath her eyes were gone, replaced by the soft, healthy glow of a woman who was finally, truly, at peace. Her other hand rested on the gentle, pronounced curve of her abdomen, a gesture of unconscious, maternal grace that sent a now-familiar wave of fierce, protective tenderness through me.

The change in my wife since she had trusted me with her truth had been nothing short of a miracle. The pale, haunted ghost who had drifted through the halls of Redwyck House was gone. In her place was this woman, a creature of quiet strength, of gentle humor, and of a warmth that had completely thawed the last of my own internal winter.

Marietta stirred beside me, a soft, sleepy sound. She shifted, her head lifting from my shoulder. She blinked, her green eyes still hazy with sleep.

"Are we almost home?" she murmured, her voice a warm, husky thing.

"Another hour, perhaps," I said softly. I reached out and brushed a stray lock of hair from her cheek, my fingers lingering on the soft, warm skin. "You should have slept longer."

She smiled, a slow, genuine smile that still had the power to stop my heart. "I am not tired. Only... content." She settled back against the velvet squabs, her hand finding mine and lacing her fingers through my own. We rode on in a comfortable, easy silence, the rhythmic clatter of the carriage wheels a peaceful, hypnotic sound. The tension of our first journeys was now a shared and precious peace.

The love I felt for her was no longer a terrifying, new thing. It had become the very foundation of my world, a quiet, steady, and unshakeable certainty. She had not just healed me; she had remade me. She had taught me how to be a man again, not just a Duke.

As the carriage swayed, my other hand came to rest on her pregnant belly, a gesture that had become as natural to me as breathing. I felt the faint, fluttering movement beneath my palm, the stirrings of my son, our son. The doctor had confirmed it last month. A boy. An heir. But the title, the lineage, the continuation of the Redwyck name—it all felt secondary now. He was not just an heir. He was our child. A symbol not of duty, but of a love I had never believed I would find.

She turned to me, her eyes dark with a sudden, profound emotion. "Thank you, Callum," she whispered.

"For what?" I asked, my brow furrowed in confusion.

"For this," she said, her voice thick. "For bringing me back to life."

The simple, profound gratitude in her words was a humbling thing. "It is you, Marietta," I said, my own voice a low, rough thing, "who has brought me back to life."

And in the warm, swaying cocoon of the carriage, with the spring landscape rushing by, I leaned in and kissed her. It was a kiss of profound, settled, and deeply contented love. His lips were soft and sure on mine, a familiar, beloved territory. The child within her gave a sudden, strong kick, a tangible, miraculous flutter against my palm.

I broke the kiss, a low, awestruck sound rumbling in my chest. I looked down at my hand on her belly, and then up at her, my grey eyes shining with a wonder and a joy so profound it took my breath away.

"He is impatient to meet his mother," I murmured, my smile a slow, beautiful thing that transformed my entire face.

"No, I think he is eager t to meet his father," she countered softly, her own heart so full of love for this man, for the family we were building, that I felt it might burst.

I looked at her, my own heart aching with a love so profound it was a physical weight in my chest. "Then it is a good thing we will both be here to greet him," I said, my voice thick with an emotion I could no longer hide.

I leaned my head down, my lips brushing against the warm silk covering her belly. "Do you hear that, little one?" I whispered to our son. "Your father is most impatient to make your acquaintance."

Marietta's soft laughter was a beautiful sound. "You might tell him yourself, Your Grace. I believe he can hear you."

I lifted my head, a slow, wicked smile spreading across my face as I met her sparkling green eyes. I leaned in close, my lips finding the shell of her ear. "Oh, I intend to get much closer than this, Duchess," I murmured, my voice a low, suggestive rumble. "And very soon."

She gasped, a lovely flush rising on her cheeks, and her fingers found my arm and gave it a light, playful pinch. "Callum!"

A low, warm chuckle rumbled in my chest. I captured her hand and brought it to my lips, kissing her fingertips. "I must confess, I have grown rather fond of that thin silk night rail you wore the other evening," I murmured, my voice a low, suggestive rumble. "You are, of course, welcome to wear it again tonight. Though my preference, Duchess, would be for you to wear nothing at all."

Her flush deepened, but her eyes sparkled with mischief. "The mouth on the future father of my child is shockingly improper," she whispered back, giving my arm another gentle pinch. "You must remember, Your Grace, there will soon be a baby in the nursery. We must set a better example."

A low, warm chuckle rumbled in my chest. I captured her hand and brought it to my lips, kissing her fingertips. My other hand came to rest on the warm, firm swell of her abdomen, a silent, possessive gesture that had become as natural as breathing.

"A few more months, my love," I murmured, my palm spreading over the life we had created. "And then our son will be here to hold us to account. Until then..." I leaned in, capturing her lips in a kiss that was deeper now, hotter, no longer just a tease but a promise of the passion that still simmered between us. "...I intend to be a very poor example indeed."

She gasped into my mouth, her own hands coming up to cup my face, pulling me closer. The kiss was all-consuming. My hand slid from her belly, moving upwards, my thumb tracing the curve of her breast over the silk of her gown. She arched against my touch, a low, helpless moan vibrating from her throat into mine.

"Callum," she breathed, breaking the kiss for a moment, her eyes dark and hazy with desire. "The carriage... it is still moving."

I looked at her, at this beautiful, passionate woman who was my wife, and I knew the rest of the journey back to London would be an agony of waiting. I would not wait.

I leaned forward and knocked sharply on the roof. "Stop the carriage here, Thomas!" I called out, my voice a firm, clear command. "And wait for my signal."

The carriage rocked to a gentle halt in a secluded stretch of the country road, surrounded by the shade of ancient oaks. In the sudden, profound quiet, there was only the sound of our ragged breathing. Marietta looked at me, a question in her eyes. I answered it by kissing her again, this time with a slow, deliberate thoroughness that left no room for doubt.

We were a husband and wife, a family being forged in the heart of a rolling carriage. Let the world outside wait. The rest of this journey was for us. The carriage began to sway with a new, urgent rhythm, and the quiet of the afternoon was filled with the sound of whispered promises and soft, breathless sighs.

We were not a scandal. We were not a secret to be hidden away. We were a family, finally, blessedly, beginning.

* * *

End of Book Two

36

Epilogue

Callum

The letter arrived on a Tuesday, an otherwise unremarkable day that had been filled with the quiet, domestic peace that had become the new rhythm of our lives. The late winter sun, a pale, hopeful thing, streamed through the windows of my study, illuminating the faint haze of dust motes dancing in the air. I was at my desk, a stack of estate papers before me, but my attention was not on the dry accounts of crop yields and tenant rents.

Through the open doorway, I could hear the faint, beautiful sound of my wife's laughter, mingling with the higher, childish peals of Isabelle. They were in the morning room, engaged in a serious and, from the sounds of it, hilarious negotiation over which doll would be permitted to attend a tea party. The sound was the backdrop to my life now, a constant, gentle melody that had soothed the last of the angry, silent ghosts of my past.

Marietta is heavily pregnant, her body full and radiant with the new life she carried. She was a vision of serene, maternal beauty, and my love for her, a thing I had once teared as a weakness, had become the central, unshakeable pillar of my existence. We were happy. It was a simple, profound, and still slightly startling fact. We were a family.

The footman entered, his movements as silent and as unobtrusive as ever. "The afternoon post, Your Grace."

He placed a small stack of letters, bound in a silk ribbon, on the corner of my desk and retreated. I glanced at them without much interest. The usual collection of political correspondence, invitations, and requests for patronage. I began to sort through them, my mind still half on the sound of my daughter's infectious giggles from down the hall.

And then I saw it.

It was a single, thin envelope, tucked at the bottom of the stack. It was made of cheap, flimsy paper, a stark contrast to the thick, cream-colored cardstock of the other letters. There was no crest on the wax seal, which was a crude, anonymous blob of dark red. The address was written in a spidery, unfamiliar hand: *To His Grace, The Duke of Highmoor. A Matter of a Private & Delicate Nature.*

A faint, almost imperceptible prickle of unease tightened the muscles in my neck. It was the instinct of a man who had spent his life navigating the treacherous currents of power and intrigue, a sense that a single, discordant note had just been struck in the otherwise perfect harmony of my day.

I slit the seal with my letter opener, the cheap wax crumbling under the blade. I unfolded the single sheet of paper within. The handwriting was the same as on the envelope, the ink a faded, brownish color. The letter was brief, its tone a strange and unsettling mixture of obsequiousness and a barely veiled threat.

Your Grace,

Pray forgive this unsolicited intrusion. I write to you as a distant cousin of the late, and much-lamented, poet, Mr. Julian Thorne. It has come to my attention, through the quiet but persistent channels of rumor, that Your Grace has recently taken a... scholarly interest in the life and works of my departed kinsman.

I find myself, by a stroke of fortune, the executor of his meager literary estate. It consists of little more than a few volumes of unsold poetry and a rather extensive collection of his private journals.

These journals, I must confess, are of a most... revealing nature. Mr. Thorne was a man of great passion and little discretion, and he chronicled his affairs of the heart with a poet's eye for detail. His liaison with a certain young lady of noble birth, a Miss G—, is of particular interest. He writes at great length of their time together, of his profound love for her, and of his deep and abiding grief over the "lost daughter" their union produced.

It occurs to me that such journals, in the wrong hands, could be the source of a most unfortunate and public scandal. In the right hands, however, they might be considered a valuable historical artifact, an asset to be protected and preserved, worthy of a significant gesture of... generosity from a party who wishes to see the past remain undisturbed.

I shall be in London for the next fortnight. Perhaps we might arrange a meeting to discuss the matter further. I am certain we can come to a mutually beneficial arrangement.

Your Grace's Most Humble & Obedient Servant,

A Friend to Poetry

I read the letter once, my blood turning to a slow, cold sludge in my veins. I read it a second time, and the words on the page seemed to writhe like venomous snakes. The quiet peace of the afternoon was shattered, replaced by the familiar, cold roar of an impending battle.

The ghost. The one I had believed vanquished, the one whose power had been neutralized by the simple, brutal fact of his death, had risen from its unmarked grave. And it had left behind a weapon.

Secret journals. A lost daughter.

The past was not dead. It had simply been waiting, a loaded pistol in the hands of a faceless blackmailer.

I looked up from the letter, my gaze falling on the open doorway of my study. The sound of my wife's laughter, which had been a source of such profound, simple joy only moments before, now sounded fragile, breakable. The beautiful, peaceful world we had so carefully, so painfully, built together was no longer a sanctuary. It was a target.

The letter lay on my desk, a declaration of war. The threat was no longer a thing of internal secrets and private griefs. It was now a real, tangible, and public danger, a scandal of catastrophic proportions waiting to explode, threatening to destroy not just my name, not just Marietta's fragile peace, but the future of our two innocent children.

I slowly, deliberately, folded the letter and held it to the flame of the candle on my desk. I watched as the cheap paper curled, blackened, and turned to ash, but I knew I could not burn away the truth it contained. The war I thought I had won was far from over. It had simply found a new, more dangerous battlefield.

37

What to look forward to in Book Three

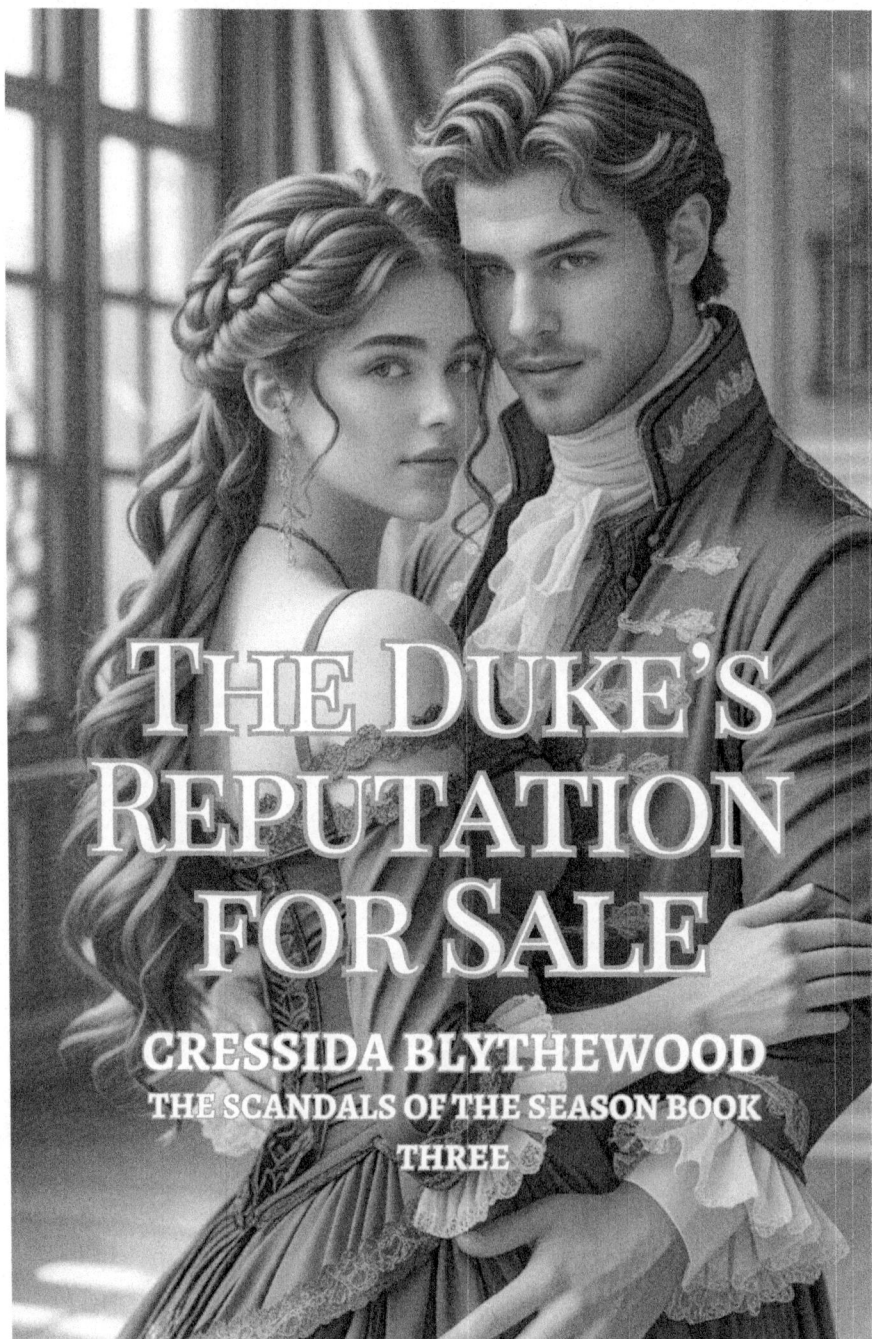

THE DUKE'S REPUTATION FOR SALE

CRESSIDA BLYTHEWOOD
THE SCANDALS OF THE SEASON BOOK THREE

They have found love in the ashes of a scandal. But the past is not finished with them.

Marietta, Duchess of Redwyck, has finally found a safe harbor in the arms of her husband, the formidable Duke Callum Redwyck. Their fragile family—built on hard-won truths and the promise of their new child—is a sanctuary against the cruelties of the world. But a sanctuary is no defense against a ghost.

A letter arrives, penned by a stranger who claims to possess the one weapon that could destroy them all: the lost journals of the poet Julian Thorne. Within their pages lies not just the story of a scandalous affair, but the truth of a secret birth—the explosive truth of Isabelle's identity.

The price of silence is steep, but the cost of revelation is unthinkable: a scandal that would not only shatter their family's honor but condemn an innocent child to a life of public shame. Forced to confront the ghosts they thought they had buried, Callum and Marietta must now wage a new war—not against each other, but against a world that feeds on secrets.

Can their newfound love withstand the poison of the past, or will the final, most devastating scandal be the one that tears them apart forever?

Coming really soon, please wait...

Printed in Dunstable, United Kingdom

70775297R00117